Over Our Heads Under Our Feet

Stories

Dwight Holing

Jackdaw Press

Over Our Heads Under Our Feet

Print Edition
Copyright 2017 by Dwight Holing
All Rights Reserved

To learn more about this author visit dwightholing.com.

ISBN: 978-0-9991468-1-1

For Annie

About the Author

Dwight Holing lives and writes in California. His collection of short fiction, *California Works: Stories*, won the 2012 Serena McDonald Kennedy Award and featured "Gallopers," winner of the 2011 Arts & Letters Prize for Fiction. His popular Jack McCoul mystery series includes *A Boatload, Bad Karma, Baby Blue,* and *Shake City.* His nonfiction work includes numerous books and articles.

For more information

Learn: dwightholing.com
Follow: @DwightHoling
Like: facebook.com/dwight.holing

Over Our Heads Under Our Feet

Stories

Stories

Over Our Heads Under Our Feet   1

The Test   23

Natural Selection   39

Between Wind and Water   48

The Things You Leave Behind   72

Desperados   81

When Mountains Melt   103

Fish Rap   109

Yellow Dog   115

Thief in the Night   134

A Special Note from the Author   149

Acclaim   150

OVER OUR HEADS UNDER OUR FEET

The lie lay between them, there in the double bed beneath a red Maasai blanket, beneath the canvas ceiling, beneath the African moon dissolving into dawn. Outside, a lion prowled the tall grass roaring impatiently for his huntresses. The ground trembled from elephants steered by memories passed on by those who had passed by before. A go-away bird's cry sounded like a petulant child. Robert listened to the Serengeti awaken, knowing that Sylvie was listening too, wishing he could reach across and pull her to him if not for the divide grown wide by the truth behind the lie.

The camp water boy finally signaled it was time to get up by singing *"jambo, jambo"* from the tent's veranda as he placed a tray of wake-up coffee and arrowroot biscuits on the outdoor table. He splashed a pail of hot water into a basin set on a folding wooden stand beneath a mirror hanging from a tree branch and called, "This shave water ready."

Robert pulled on his boots and stepped from the long night into a new day. Five other tents formed a crescent on the crest of a rise overlooking the savannah. A canvas village housing the kitchen and camp staff was pitched a discreet distance away in a stand of yellow fever trees. He sipped the silty coffee and marveled at the illusion of permanence. None of it was here a few days ago, and it would only be here as long as the main herds of wildebeest, zebras, and gazelles kept marching toward the Mara River and braved crocodiles and drowning to reach the fresh graze on the Kenyan side. When the waves of animals dwindled down to the old and the lame, the tents would be struck and swept up in the journey, as much a part of the great migration as the prey leading and the predators following, their speed and direction dictated by sun and rain, birth and death. Only dust and memories would remain, and even those would fade with time.

He left the binoculars hanging from his neck as he scanned the savannah for movement. Flat-topped acacia trees studded the sea of grass, and the bulbous trunks of the baobabs looked like zeppelins plunged to Earth. Robert spotted a trio of ostriches not fifty feet away. Two males flushed pink to signal their virility were jousting over a drab female who seemed more interested in pecking the ground for locusts still sluggish with dew than mating. A family of warthogs scurried into the tall grass to get out of their way, the four piglets chasing after the big-teated sow, her upraised tail with its tuft of coarse bristles signaling the same as a tour guide's umbrella. Overhead, the stars grew as faint as grains of salt poured on a glass table then blown quietly and steadily away. He sensed the planet's spin beneath his feet, felt the Serengeti move to take its rightful turn in the sun, carrying him further from home and all that he knew.

It was Sylvie's suggestion to go on safari, but Robert didn't need any convincing. A once-in-a-lifetime adventure, she kept calling it, clinging as if to a mantra the same words printed in bold on the homepage of the outfitter's website. A distraction was what she really meant, but Robert didn't say that out loud. Since his diagnosis, he avoided saying things like "bucket list" around her, sticking to the lie they told themselves, rarely giving into gallows humor—*rire jaune*, as she called it. He smiled at that. Even the grim sounded pretty in her native tongue.

Robert had always wanted to come to Africa, just never had made the time, his surgery practice demanding, his travel usually restricted to medical conferences. Whenever he did take a trip, he always packed his binoculars for birding, a pastime he'd picked up in college to break the monotony of stuffy classrooms and hours hunkered in windowless labs. The species he spotted were usually of common variety, but no matter if robin, sparrow, or jay, each was confirmation that he was part of a life much bigger, more enduring than his could ever be.

Now the birdsong surrounding him rose to a febrile pitch as the sky lightened, illuminating insects to be snapped up, flowers to sip, rodents to hunt, and carcasses to scavenge. Robert closed his eyes and tried to distinguish the monkey-like chatter of a white-browed coucal from the rising coo of a laughing dove, the stutter of a superb starling showing off its iridescent beauty to a prospective mate. He had done his homework before coming, bought all the field guides on East African birds he could find, downloaded recordings off the internet, listened to them instead of dosing himself with Ambien for the 25-hour flight from San Francisco. He'd set a goal of seeing 200 new species the three weeks he'd be in Tanzania. It wasn't too ambitious considering how many inhabited this part of the world, and he was well on his way to achieving it, perhaps even eclipsing it. Each new sighting earned a checkmark and notation on a list he carried in the front pocket of his khaki safari vest. He went over it each night to test himself, an exercise he conducted with the same attention he gave to reciting favorite quotes he'd memorized, like Thoreau's "Heaven is under our feet as well as over our heads." Remembering the words, saying them in order, was a way to gauge the progress of the disease, the "slow slide" as he dismissed his early-onset dementia, the sobriquet an attempt to keep at arms distance that which his medical degree and practice had made him no less immune to than a day laborer, a carpenter, a cop.

Opening his eyes again, Robert spotted a flutter atop a distant candelabra tree and raised his binoculars, hoping to see a bird that still eluded him, the pale chanting goshawk. His field guide described it as a beautiful, sleek-winged raptor with a haunting, lyrical call that hunted in the air as well as on the ground. What intrigued him was its triangular mating behavior to ensure breeding success, one of the few polyandrous species in the animal world. The *Jules et Jim* of birds, Robert smiled to himself, thinking that's just how Sylvie would describe the males in the feathered *ménage*. But this time, it was only a gust of wind blowing some branches. And then he remembered it was time for breakfast.

"They'll be serving soon," he called over his shoulder. "Are you about ready?"

Sylvie's reply was muffled, nearly drowned in a swaddling of soft cotton sheets. "Not quite."

Robert didn't need to turn around to see her, the way her hair framed her face no matter if tousled by sleep or newly cut, the way her eyes sparkled with laughter or flashed with anger, smoldered during sex or glistened with tears. So far, he didn't have to work at it to keep Sylvie's image branded in his memory like he did with so many others. Or at least he told himself so. Again, the power of the lie. It protected him from losing control, what he feared above all—the day he saw her but didn't, the day he looked into the mirror and couldn't place the man with the shaving cream on his jaw, a toothbrush in his hand.

"You want me to wait?" he asked.

Sylvie sucked in her breath before blowing it out as if to extinguish what could never be. "Go ahead," she finally said. "I'll be along."

*

The head guide was named Justice and his second called himself Goodluck. They were standing by the campfire sipping tea from bone china cups and saucers with a cabbage rose pattern. Flames licked dried sticks that the campfire tender had gathered from beneath a nearby sausage tree. He had been extra careful in his selection after a story spread like the lightening-strike blazes that hopscotched across the grasslands. Another tender had been bitten by a black mamba that had slithered into the woodpile during the night. The cook had run over at the sound of his screams and hacked off the poisoned hand to stop the flow of fatal venom. Now at campfire pits throughout the park sticks were placed in the shape of a cross, a crescent, or the horns of a cow, depending on the tender's religion.

Goodluck greeted Robert with a toothy smile. "*Jambo?*" No matter if he was speaking Swahili or English, the lanky, good-natured guide always sounded as if he were asking a question.

Robert returned the greeting and then said good morning to Justice, the older and more experienced of the two. Both men came from the highlands of Mount Meru, Kilimanjaro's little sister, but they lived in different villages and belonged to different tribes, prayed to different gods.

"Good morning, Doctor. How did you sleep the night?" Justice asked in his quiet, deliberate way.

"Like a baby." He smiled, indulging himself a little in Sylvie's absence.

The African's liquid brown eyes washed over him and Robert got the feeling that Justice saw right through him, that eventually, he'd ask about the lie. To put him off, he said, "Any chance I'll get my pale chanting today?"

The guide paused. He was stocky, his shaved round skull absorbing the morning sun like a black hole swallowing starlight. "It is possible, but it is up to the chanting. Today we hope for the leopard. There is a kopje with many trees by the river. It is a good place for this leopard. He watch for the impala there. This leopard like the impala very much. It is of proper size. He carry the impala up the tree to keep from the hyena. You like this place very much."

Two men walked into camp from the grassy plain. Colin was a freelance photographer hired by the outfitter to capture images for the website. He sported a week of stubble that matched his war correspondent's attire and air of confident indifference. A pair of cameras dangled from his neck on black neoprene straps. Imani followed a few steps behind. The Maasai wore a red blanket over his shoulders and hoop earrings strung with white cowry shells and trade beads. Strips cut from motorcycle tires were strapped to his narrow feet. The metal tip of his spear was the shape of a heart. Earlier, Colin had told Robert and Sylvie the story of how Imani killed a lion attacking his family's cattle when he was just a boy, said when he was out shooting pictures in the bush he wouldn't trade the Maasai and his spear for a half dozen big game hunters.

"See anything special?" Robert asked.

Colin accepted a coffee from the dining steward and took a moment to hold the delicate cup to his chin and inhale the curling steam. Brows that formed wings the color of a tawny eagle's hooded his pale eyes. "We tracked a herd of giraffes through the night and shot them silhouetted against the rising sun. Brilliant." He had some kind of accent, but Robert forgot where he was from. It wasn't Australia or South Africa, that much he was sure of. Well, pretty sure of, anyway. "We were courtside to a pack of hunting dogs chasing down a hartebeest. Very efficient those dogs."

"But you won't be able to use that for advertising, will you? The kill shot, that is," Sylvie said as she approached their circle.

The men turned to greet her. She was wearing a baseball cap, and her short blonde ponytail was pulled through the opening above the strap. A silk scarf the color of tall grass turned in summer wrapped her long neck.

Colin didn't try to hide his smile as she slipped between him and Robert. "Quite right," he said. "Too unambiguous."

"Show me."

The photographer set his coffee down, raised one of the cameras, eyed the LCD monitor, and sidled closer. Sylvie didn't flinch as he held it up for her to view the sequence of shots showing the hartebeest being ripped apart.

"Beautiful even in death," she said.

"The hartebeest," he said.

"That too," she said.

Robert watched his wife and the photographer, noted their restraint, heard their unspoken words, but then his thoughts turned to the deer-sized antelope with the caliper-shaped horns. He wondered if it ever considered giving up during the chase, if it clung to hope that it could still escape as the pack of calico dogs disemboweled it, pulled its entrails out in strings, gorged on its liver, chewed its heart while it still beat. When did the poor creature finally give over to the embrace of earth warmed by its own blood?

Justice looked up from his tea, the tiny cup and saucer looking all the more fragile in his calloused and capable hands. "This hartebeest eat the grass and the dog eat this hartebeest. Everything eat this hartebeest. The vulture eat what the dog leave behind. The hyena eat the bone. And the tortoise eat the hyena dung. Nothing of this hartebeest is to waste."

*

They set out after breakfast in three royal blue Land Cruisers with a rhino's profile painted in white on the front doors. Goodluck drove two other couples. The Liggets hailed from a wealthy suburb of Houston, the husband's drawl and opinions seasoned by single mash and cigar smoke, the wife always saying the shows she watched on *Animal Planet* never mentioned anything about flies. The Matsuis lived in Tokyo and dressed like beekeepers to ward off the equatorial sun. Their English was limited to what they'd heard on CNN and learned online. A young guide-in-training drove the Custodies, a family of four from New Jersey. The parents spent most of their time shepherding the kids and explaining away their behavior. The daughter was in her early teens and sunbathed in a bikini even though Justice told her parents that it made the Muslim members of the staff uncomfortable. The son was much younger and had developed a case of hero worship and pointed his silver automatic camera wherever Colin aimed his big telephoto lens, wore a scarf he borrowed from his mother like the photographer's black and white checked keffiyeh.

Robert sat in the front seat of the lead vehicle next to Justice who kicked his sandals off when he drove. The head guide's soles were hardened, his toenails like overwaxed floor tiles. He never stopped looking for animals no matter how rugged the road, how much the Land Cruiser bounced. It was as if his head was mounted on a gimbal. Sylvie and Colin stood on the back seat, their head and shoulders above the sunroof, their knees bent to absorb the bumpy dirt track with deep ruts carved during the rainy season. Robert pictured the wide plain of green grass as the open ocean, saw his wife and the photographer zipping across it on sailboards, the wind blowing their hair, a chain of tropical islands glimmering on the far horizon. Then he remembered. After the safari, they were going to Zanzibar to wash the dust off at a beach resort. He'd be able to look for seabirds there and add to his list while she swam in the turquoise sea, lay on the white sand beach. He tried to recall the coastal section in the field guide, sifted through the pictures and names he'd filed away. Crab plovers, black winged stilts, a curlew of some kind, the exact name floating maddeningly just beyond his reach.

Justice downshifted and brought the three-ton vehicle shuddering to a stop. Robert snapped back to the moment, followed the African's gaze, knowing by now he had a sixth sense when it came to spotting wildlife, no matter how far the distance, how perfect their camouflage. His pulse quickened as he readied his binoculars. "Is it my pale chanting? Where?"

"It is the lilac-breasted roller. There." Justice pointed a stubby finger at the top of a nearby acacia. "Watch. You like this bird very much."

Robert thumbed the focus wheel and two birds filled the glass. The pair perched on the tip of a branch. Both had turquoise wings and their downy breasts were the color of French lavender, Sylvie's favorite flower. He pictured the cut bunches that she bought from sidewalk vendors stationed outside the downtown office building where she worked to fill the vases in their Pacific Heights flat, the live ones she grew in the terracotta pots on their deck with the sweeping view of the Golden Gate. He could hear her coo to them as she snipped and watered. *Mes enfants. Jolis bébés.* Until his diagnosis, he'd never regretted not having children. No time for them, he always told himself, too busy running the surgery department, seeing patients, saving lives. But now that he'd slid into the in-between time, slowly losing his past and not wanting to see his future, he wished for someone to be there, not to help take care of him, feed him, wipe his lips, his ass—he had a plan for that—but to be there for her, Sylvie ten years younger than he. Robert glanced at the rearview mirror, seeing her perched there, the photographer too.

"You see it?" Justice asked. "Watch this roller now."

Robert refocused his binoculars. One of the birds suddenly springboarded off the supple branch, swooping right at them then pulling up, using the momentum to slingshot skyward, its wings tucked in, its tail straight back. The bird zoomed up until gravity reclaimed control. Stalling, the roller pitched forward, cartwheeling as it plummeted, its feathers flashing like shards of colored glass trapped inside a kaleidoscope. Just before it crashed the bird pulled out and hopped back on the branch next to the other roller.

"The lilac-breasted roller mate until the end of time," said Justice, nodding as he explained it. "This male dance for this female to show he still strong. He dance for this other male watching and waiting in this tree to show he still strong."

*

That evening they sat in canvas folding chairs circled around the campfire. The dining steward had freshened after-dinner drinks, and Robert was nursing a tumbler of whisky as he conducted a mental exercise, carefully retracing the steps the kitchen crew took to ensure there was always enough ice even though their only refrigeration was powered by a portable solar panel. Sparks were shooting from the fire and joining the flicker of constellations he did not recognize when Ligget started grumbling that if Goodluck hadn't flanked the kopje instead of driving straight up to it as Justice had he wouldn't have missed seeing the leopard.

"Our boy's people misnamed him," the Texan drawled. "From now on I'm gonna start callin' him Badluck."

Sylvie glanced over at the dining tent where the guides were discussing plans for the next day's game drive before turning back to Ligget, her smile anything but. "People always want to end my name with an *a*. Does anyone ever start yours with a *B*?"

Ligget's jowls reddened even more than they already were

from the campfire, but then he slapped his knee and laughed. "Well, hell, *mademoiselle*, I expect I had that comin'." He winked at Sylvie then jabbed his bourbon in the direction of the dining tent. "Hey, Goodluck. Y'all all right, ya hear?" He grinned at the others. "Guess there's plenty of kitty cats left to see, am I right, Doc? How 'bout it, Paparazzi? We gonna spot more?"

The tension discharged, the murmur of small talk rushed in. But Robert knew Sylvie wouldn't let go of Ligget's slur so easily, that she'd keep it bottled inside her along with the fear, the anger, and, most of all, the guilt she'd been holding onto ever since he told her the results of the tests he'd undergone following a series of troubling episodes. They started when he couldn't find his car in the hospital garage, a morning in the operating room when he had forgotten to wear his scrubs. When he had explained to Sylvie what they could expect, he described the sand castles he used to build on vacations with his parents, the carefully excavated moats catching but never stopping the ocean, each subsequent lap of foamy water slowly rounding the angular defense walls that he had patted painstakingly into place, the inevitable collapse of battlements, towers, and keep, the remaining hump of sand finally erased like birdcalls blown on the wind. As he spoke, he could see in her eyes that she would exchange if she could the slow and steady creep of the tide for the shock and surprise of one big wave. And that in wanting what she could never admit to herself, the lie was born.

Robert leaned across Sylvie and said to Colin, "Are you going out to take pictures tonight?"

The photographer, balancing a whisky on his knee, his chin buried in the folds of his keffiyeh, kept his gaze on the glowing embers. "I expect so. Would you care to accompany me?"

The invitation surprised him. "I didn't think it was allowed. The guides instructed us never to leave the camp, especially after dark. Even after dinner, they escort us back to our tents."

Colin shrugged. "You are paying a great deal of money for this adventure, Doctor. I will speak to Justice. We shall take the necessary precautions." He turned to Sylvie. "Perhaps you would care to come as well. You would find it interesting. Exciting, I should think. The Serengeti is an entirely different world at night. There are as many eyes glowing around you as there are stars shining above. Your senses become keener in the dark. The slightest sound ignites your imagination. The slightest touch, whether it's a breeze tugging at your blouse or your companion brushing up against you, sends your blood racing, your heart pounding, everything quivering with the expectation of danger and ultimately glorious release."

Robert waited for Sylvie's reply, thinking about what it would be like to walk alone into the dark, straight into the roars and yelps and trumpeting that pierced the pooling black night, to leave the safety of lights and voices and everything he knew behind. To go to a place where the slow slide could not follow.

But she stood abruptly and said curtly, "Maybe tomorrow." She put her hand on Robert's shoulder. "I'm going to turn in. Coming?"

Imani, as if by magic, was suddenly standing right behind them. The Maasai held his warrior's spear in one hand, a flashlight in the other. He waited for Robert to join her then began walking toward their tent, his footsteps silent on the matted trail, training the beam behind him so they could stay within the pale wafer of safety as another member of the camp wordlessly brought up the rear, a rifle slung over his shoulder.

When they reached their tent, Sylvie unzipped the bug screen and bid their escorts the traditional Swahili wish for sweet dreams. *"Lala salama,"* she said.

A single bulb hanging from the ceiling gave the tent a candlelight glow. They undressed and slipped between the freshly laundered sheets that still held the warmth of the sun under which they had dried. Robert went over his bird list, racing the dimming light as the charge drained from its solar-powered battery.

"What did you make of Colin's offer?" he asked as he silently counted and recounted the checkmarks, questioning their accuracy as if a faulty pen stroke could be to blame for the bird sightings he could not recall.

Sylvie lay on her side, her face turned toward him, the red Maasai blanket humped like the savannah's termite mounds that had been rounded by wind and rain. "I really didn't give it much thought."

"His invitation sounded genuine enough."

"I'm sure it was." Her voice sounded weary.

"It would be an incredible experience. The highlight of the trip."

"Uh huh," she murmured.

"Good. Then it's settled. You'll go tomorrow night."

"Me?" That brought her to an elbow. "What are you talking about?"

"Colin said he could guarantee your safety. He's a good man. I trust him."

Exasperation weighed her sigh. "And you think I'd go by myself, without you."

"I think you should go. I want you to. Besides, there's no chance for me to see a pale chanting in the dark."

"That's no excuse and you know it," she said.

Robert paused and took a breath as he faced down the lie. "All right. You know I can't. The Sundowners."

He said it matter-of-factly, applying another sobriquet to take the sting out of the disorienting syndrome that struck after darkness fell, when all the reference points that guided him clicked off like the instrument gauges in a cockpit. Last night he had awakened to find Sylvie straddling him, her thighs pinning his hips, her fingers clamping his wrists to the mattress. Her lips were inches from his, her breath coming in loud, labored gasps as she held him down. He could feel the heat coming off her like the afternoon gusts that sent the grasslands galloping, could feel the quickening thump of her heart. But what he could not feel was himself inside her, her warm sex around his. And then he heard the echo of a voice he did not recognize, the pleading angry, the words ringing with frustration. *Let me go. I just want to go downstairs and get a snack, watch some TV. Let me go, dammit.*

Robert's blunt admission left no room for pretending. Sylvie raised her chin. "All the more reason why I won't go, can't go."

He put the bird list down, adopted Colin's accent: "We shall take the necessary precautions, I should think. Imani and his spear, me and mine, you shall find it fascinating."

The corners of Sylvie's frown turned slightly. Encouraged, Robert kept at it, seeing her now like he did all those years ago when they had first met. It was at some civic event or a fundraiser or a lecture, he couldn't remember which, but what he couldn't forget, hoped never to forget, was how he couldn't take his eyes off her, how beautiful her smile, how she laughed at the little jokes he made across the table, how afterward she told her friends it was his humor, not hormones, that had swept her off her feet.

He went back to his own voice, going for a playful tone. "You needn't worry about me. I'll wear my reading headlamp all night long and keep both flashlights on. I'll tie my ankles to the bed with my belt. The worst that can happen is I get up and trip and get a bloody lip. They'll find me trussed up in the morning, start a whisper campaign about the San Franciscans who are into B and D."

Sylvie laughed, but the longer he went on the more her eyes and smile began to leak. She was so tired, so awfully tired. It was all she could do to pat him on the shoulder and wish themselves *lala salama*, as if such things were still possible.

*

In the morning, Justice had the camp water boy rouse the camp earlier than usual. An enormous herd of wildebeest was crowding the savannah, the smell of the Mara River causing the animals to close ranks and gather speed, the air thickening with the sounds of pounding hooves and panicky bullfrog-like grunts.

"You like this river crossing very much," Justice said as they ate a hurried breakfast of biscuits and marmalade, rushing to load into the Land Cruisers. "This crossing very *National Geographic*."

The drivers took the dirt track faster than usual to get ahead of the herd. Imani rode up front with Justice to keep an eye out for lions. A herd on the move brought out all the predators. Sylvie sat between Robert and Colin in the backseat, the three bracing against each other as the speeding Land Cruiser pitched and yawed. Dust motes danced on the sunlight streaming through the open roof, but no one dared speak lest the bouncing cause them to bite their tongues. They crested a rise and the brown waters of the Mara roiled below. Justice parked the royal blue four-by on a decline to give them a birds-eye view. The other vehicles pulled alongside. The river looked to Robert like a python undulating through the tall grass.

"Look," Justice said, his usual deliberateness giving way to hurry. "The wildebeest coming very fast now. You say a stampede, yes?" He nodded to himself. "You like this stampede very much."

Sylvie stood on the seat. Robert joined her. So did Colin. The photographer set a black nylon bag filled with grains of uncooked rice on the edge of the opened roof and used it as a makeshift brace for his telephoto lens. Within moments they were surrounded by snorting animals, the herd moving like the river itself, forking around the three vehicles then merging back into a single, unstoppable flow. There was no hesitation now. Even if the lead animals wanted to stop, they could not, for the powerful surge behind them pushed relentlessly onward. The brown water churned as the first wildebeest leapt off the bank. More followed. The rapids swept some downstream. Others were shoved underwater as new jumpers landed on top. Cauldrons frothed and water mushrooms sprouted as unblinking crocodiles grabbed flailing legs and pulled their victims under. Those lucky enough to make it across scrambled up a steep, muddy bank. It was a pandemonic scrum. Hooves twisted. Legs snapped. Ribs cracked.

"Reminds me of the lemmings I photographed in Lapland," Colin said above the whine of his camera's motor drive and the pitiful bleats of panicking animals. "An uncontrollable rush to the end. As fascinating as it was frightening." And then he did what he always did on game drives and around the camp, turned his lens on Sylvie and snapped away.

For more than an hour, the herd kept coming. Robert scanned the Kenyan side of the river. The vast plain was filling fast with thousands of wildebeest. Those that had made it safely across lost little time shoving their bearded muzzles into the lush green grass. Not a single creature, not one, ever looked back, and Robert marveled at how such a momentous event that meant the difference between life and death could be forgotten so quickly.

As the sun grew hotter, the flow of wildebeest slowed to a trickle as the old and hobbling tried to keep up. One stumbled close by, knocking into the front fender of the Land Cruiser. Twin trails of snot dripped from its nostrils. Sickly yellow foam flecked its beard. Its eyes were rolled back, the wheezing animal lurching like a drunkard.

"What happened to him?" Ligget called from the open roof of his vehicle. He and Matsui were standing, their wives sitting inside. "He ain't gonna make it."

Justice had his window down. "This wildebeest has nagana. He bit by tsetse fly."

"Well, hell, then somebody oughta shoot him," the Texan said. "Put the poor bastard out of his misery. That's what we'd do back home."

Textbooks scrolled through Robert's mind, slides from a distant lecture flashed. "I thought wild animals were immune to sleeping sickness," he said.

"Yes, this is correct mostly." The guide glanced at Imani. "But this wildebeest he eat the grass close to Maasai cattle eating the grass. This cattle sacred to Maasai, but tsetse bite Maasai cattle and many die from nagana until the end of time."

Ligget shook his head. "We got a gun for lions in the truck, right? Somebody oughta use it. If it was me? I'd take a bullet over drowning or gettin' eaten by gators any damn day of the week. Am I right, Doc? Y'all with me, Paparazzi?"

Justice spoke before either could answer. "This journey is this wildebeest journey. This journey end the way it supposed to end. Here in Tanzania or there in Kenya. In the water or in the belly of crocodile. This wildebeest journey not for us to decide."

He started the engine and slowly backed up, moving away from the sick creature. When they were clear of it, he turned around and followed the track back to camp.

*

After lunch they retired to their tents to wait out the heat of the day. Sylvie requested a shower, and the camp water boy fetched a five-gallon pail warmed on the kitchen fire. He attached it to a rope strung through a pulley and hoisted it to the top of the shower stall, a tarped enclosure attached to the back of their tent and accessible through a zippered pass-through. Then he deftly tipped the pail, so it filled a basin affixed to a gravity-fed showerhead.

"This shower water ready," he sang out.

"*Asante sana*," Sylvie sang back.

Robert was stretched out on the red Maasai blanket going over his bird list. Sylvie undressed and placed her clothes on the foot of the bed. "Come help me wash my hair," she said.

Even in the shadowy light, he could make out the nevus flammeus on her left thigh, a small port wine stain the shape of the Little Dipper. He reached over and traced it with his fingertip. "My guiding star," he whispered.

Over the years, the line had become a private joke, and she gave the automatic roll of the eyes. "Why Doctor, I just need some help rinsing out the shampoo."

They squeezed into the tarp-walled stall, standing on a wooden grate. He pulled the dangling cord and released just enough water to wet them, saving the rest for rinsing. They soaped up then Robert took a travel-sized plastic bottle of shampoo and squeezed some on Sylvie's scalp, combing her thick tendrils with fingers that once wielded scalpels, patched patients' hearts, removed tumors, but were now powerless to fix the disease growing inside his brain. She tilted her head, raised her face to the African sky, and moaned with pleasure as he worked in the shampoo. He knew her eyes were shut, her lips parted, her tongue pressed against the back of her teeth. They knew each other as well as two people could and he realized that's what he would miss most of all.

"Colin is going on a photo safari tonight," he said. "He told me there's bound to be plenty of cats looking for stragglers. Not just lions, but the smaller, harder to see ones. Servals, civets, and, and..." He halted, the name as slippery as the bar of soap.

"Caracals," she prompted.

"Yes, those too." He was unable to keep the frustration from his voice. "You're going, right?"

Sylvie turned around, her eyes flashing with impatience. "Why is this so important to you? You're being very controlling, you know, just like you are at the hospital. With everything."

"Because..." He hesitated, struggling with the words, slapped the side of his head. "Because I can't control this."

The echo in the tiny stall wrapped them tighter than the plastic walls and Sylvie started to cry. "It's so unfair. *Je déteste. Je déteste.*"

Robert slipped his arms around her, tucked her head beneath his chin. They stood there rocking gently, Robert keeping to himself what 20 years of practicing medicine had taught him, that healing always involved a combination of skill and luck, but when it came to surviving, fairness never entered the equation. He pulled the cord and released the rest of the water. It fell like warm rain, washing the soap and shampoo and tears down their bellies, down their legs, down through the slats in the wooden grate where it all disappeared into the black earth below.

*

Clouds bunched over the savannah in the late afternoon and the air turned skittish as thermals rose and dust devils careened across the plain. Gusts sent the tents billowing like lungs and the laundry hanging on lengths of manila rope tied between pairs of yellow fever trees whipped and snapped. Robert and Sylvie joined the others having four o'clock tea before the usual pre-dinner game drive. The dining steward apologized for not having any freshly baked cakes to go along with their coffee and Earl Grey, explaining that the cook couldn't risk lighting a fire beneath his cast-iron potjie.

"I think it's too windy to leave camp," Mrs. Custodie said, her eyebrows twitching.

"Yeah, we're tired of looking at dumb animals," her daughter said.

"Okay, we won't go," said the father.

"Count us out too," Ligget said. "We'll take a pass on feeding the skeeters." He pantomimed to the Matsuis to join them for cocktails and cards.

Colin turned to Sylvie and Robert. "The wind will die down by tonight. We shall be going out after dark anyway. Do you wish to wait until then?"

Robert hesitated. "What about it, Justice? Is it worth going now?"

The head guide cradled his bone china cup as if it were an egg. "This wind very good for bird watching. They do not fly high in this sky. You like this wind very much."

"Because there's a good chance I'll find my pale chanting?"

"It is always possible, but it is up to the chanting."

"That settles it. I'll go now."

"Then so will I," Sylvie said.

Robert touched her arm. "Why don't you wait for the night safari?"

She glanced at Colin then back at him. "I can do both."

He paused then nodded. "Okay. Both it is."

The photographer shrugged. "If the birds are out now, I should come to. Who knows what we might find."

The Custodies' son stomped his feet, held his silver camera out like a gun. "If Colin's going then I'm going too. You can't stop me."

His parents went into overdrive first cajoling then threatening, but after a while they gave in and agreed he could go as long as Imani went to watch after him.

Justice led the way to the lone Land Cruiser and they loaded up, the young boy sitting between Colin and Sylvie with the Maasai in the jump seat behind. Robert rode up front with Justice. A new track took them away from the Mara River and across a desolate tableland where the grass had already been grazed and the stubble charred by lightning strikes. Robert began to doubt Justice's choice of routes. Nothing appeared to be alive, nothing seemed to be moving except the wind and dust. The soil was the color of ash punctuated by heaps of bleached wildebeest bones. They passed a single horn still attached to a gazelle skull pointing straight up. It reminded him of a stick of driftwood he once spent hours trying to pull from the sand in front of his family's beach house, pretending it to be Excalibur, not knowing that it was the tip of a water-logged limb buried by a high tide.

Heat haze melted the horizon and the blue silhouette of a far-off mountain range hovered over a wavering lake that didn't exist. Thunder rolled in the distance. Robert could hear Sylvie and Colin chatting behind him, he saying he knew the city in Provence where she had been born, had gone there on a photo assignment, she saying she would love to visit New Zealand someday and asked if there were any similarities between the Maoris and the Maasai.

They were driving straight into the sun and Robert cursed himself for having forgotten his sunglasses. He squinted and turned his head, but the rays still found him, forcing his eyes closed. Red spots flamed behind the lids and he was powerless to blink or rub them away. He heard his father all these years gone warning him not to stare at an eclipse. He saw the red insides of the first chest he ever cracked, a heart-pumping lazily between layers of yellow coronary fat, blood oozing from a loosened clamp, blood draining from the face of a wife, a husband, a mother, a father standing in the waiting room as he delivered bad news about their loved one. He saw Sylvie's mouth with blood red lipstick whispering *je t'aime*.

The sun beat down. The motor droned. The front seat throbbed. And Robert felt himself falling backward through a red hole darkening into violet then blackness. The light faded and with it the details he clung to: his mother's touch, his boyhood adventures, the thrill of saving his first life, Sylvie's wedding dress, his life list of birds. The fall was finally broken by a noisy jolt and a sharp jab. He opened his eyes. The Land Cruiser had taken a hard turn, hitting a pothole, throwing him against the door. His head hurt and his limbs felt thick and heavy. He looked groggily at the driver, but the man was concentrating on keeping to the rutted track as the ashy soil turned stony, the burnt stubble giving over to thorny scrub. A silver jackal darted in front. A blue agama lizard performed pushups on a tombstone of black rock glinting with flint. A lone acacia tree led to another and then another and finally to a gathering of shiny trunks, their entwining limbs locked in embrace.

The driver took his bare foot off the gas but did not apply the brakes. He turned the ignition off and they quietly rolled to a stop.

"Ahead in this tree," he whispered. "Twelve on the clock."

Robert instinctively raised his binoculars at the black branches etched against a flat and colorless sky. "What is it?" he whispered back. "What am I looking for?"

"That which you wish."

He strained against the rubber eyecups, clumsily fingering the focus wheel. And then he remembered as the glass filled with piercing yellow eyes looking right back through a mask of gray feathers. Finally, his pale chanting goshawk. And a male too. Robert held his breath as he locked eyes with the creature, afraid that even the sound of his pulse would scare it off. How perfectly it was built to live free in the wild. Strong enough to fly, light enough to float. A cunning predator and equally as cunning when it came to propagating its kind.

It was the bird that broke off the stare-down. The goshawk swiveled his head owl-like, peered at the ground, and pushed off on long, red legs. His white and dark gray barred belly blinking as he wheeled on black-tipped wings. Diving swiftly, his sharp talons outstretched, he plucked a striped ground squirrel scurrying across a pebbly clearing. The wind kicked up and sent clouds of twigs and dirt spinning like tops, but the pale raptor did not falter. With the plump prize now hanging limp in his clutch, he flapped his powerful wings and climbed.

Robert swiveled his binoculars to track the bird's flight, but the windshield's thick frame blocked his view. He yanked open the heavy door and scrambled out, leaving the vehicle behind, unmindful of stepping into a world of predator and prey, unmindful of the voices calling to him, listening only for the chant of the pale bird. He would not be denied now. He had searched for it for so long, wanted it, needed it.

The chase took him across the clearing, hurdling clumps of dried red grass, crashing through thickets of thornbush as the goshawk led him. On the far side of the clearing, the bird slowed and circled the crown of a tall flat-topped acacia. Arching his wings and dropping his tail, he hovered in mid-air then settled down on the edge of a nest made of braided twigs and dried grasses fastened atop a fanning branch. A pair of similarly plumed birds greeted the hunter with shrieks, a female and another male. And though Robert couldn't see into their nest, he was sure it held two blue eggs more fragile than bone china teacups. The hunter held out the striped ground squirrel to the female as the other male blinked his yellow eyes then bobbed his head approvingly. Robert watched as she split open the fat rodent's furry belly with her blood red beak and ate. As she did, her mates began to chant.

The warm Serengeti wind carried the haunting duet down from the treetop and across the clearing. The notes swirled around him, spinning him, slowly at first, then faster and faster, until they lifted him off the ancient ground. The chant carried him up, level to the branches of the trees, and then higher. He was soaring now, circling like his precious birds, above the plains, above the flat-topped acacias. He looked down and saw a Land Cruiser, saw a man behind the steering wheel looking on wisely, saw a shadow in the seat next to him, saw a man in a red blanket looking out for danger, saw a handsome man and a beautiful woman standing in the middle, their shoulders touching. She was boosting up a child so he could look out the open roof too, and through the long lens of a camera that the man held steady for him. The boy was asking questions and the woman was answering patiently, her voice mingling with the chanting of the goshawks.

He drifted past, his shadow slipping into the gathering dusk now, and there among the pale chantings, there beneath the African sky, he closed his eyes and no longer thought about what once was or what would be.

THE TEST

Emma's reading light glowed across the Pacific as she shuffled a thick stack of documents. They were chapters of her life as well as a ticket to the future. Medical records, bank statements, and personal character references from her Chair of the Board and Congresswoman were collated with tabs. Printouts of emails between her lawyer, the Chinese Consulate, and the Children's Welfare Agency in Jiangxi were arranged in chronological order. She would read a few pages and then return to the most prized piece of paper of all. The Referral. It bore the letterhead of the Chinese Center for Adoption Affairs at the top and a photograph of a smiling two-year-old girl at the bottom. She practiced saying the name written beneath it. Xi'an Hua. She'd looked up the translation. *Peace Flower.*

"You should catch some shut-eye," Sean said. He'd been sipping champagne and watching movies since they left San Francisco. "The time change can really screw with you."

"Thank you, Doctor." She gave the title a sisterly needle. "I need to be ready for their questions. They put you through the third degree and there's so much material to go over, so much to remember."

"They're looking for mothers, not robots."

"I don't want them to get hung up on my marital status."

"Just tell them..." Sean screwed up his face and assumed one of his film accents. "Husbands? We don't need no stinkin' husbands."

They landed in Hong Kong and checked into the Mandarin. Emma couldn't fall asleep, and not because it was morning either. She kept staring across Victoria Harbor.

"I'm coming." Her whisper fogged the hotel window. "I'm coming."

Emma and Sean met their guide the next morning. His name was Luk Tam, but he said everyone called him Lucky. His English was as laid-back as a surfer's, his hair streaked as if by sun. When he told them he'd lived in the Castro for a couple of years, Sean started naming his favorite clubs and bars there.

"I can't believe I never ran into you at Butter or on the dance floor at The Café," he said.

Lucky grinned. "Maybe you did."

Emma tried not to let her impatience show. "Can we leave for the Mainland now? I don't want them to give Xi'an Hua to someone else."

Lucky patted her wrist. "*No problema.* My cousin has it wired on the inside. Beijing knows who you are and no one's about to give themselves a black eye. Things move pretty slowly over there, so patience is our best friend. Okay, Miss B?"

They took a ferry to Shenzhen and then transferred to a flight to Nanchang. Emma sat in the window seat and stared at the countryside below. Factories gave way to farmland. Rivers snaked between mountain ranges. Smoke curled from villages.

I wonder which one Xi'an Hua comes from, she thought to herself. *I wonder if she'll love her new bedroom. Love me.*

She leaned over to her brother for reassurance, but Sean had his earbuds on and was watching a movie on his phone. Lucky was watching it too.

It was raining when they landed. They'd reserved adjoining rooms at the Lakeview Hotel. The carpet smelled musty and the bedding was clammy. The view of the city's famed four lakes was obstructed by gloomy clouds veined with coal dust. They went downstairs and found the restaurant crowded with Americans. The men were watchful. The women stared at their plates as if the food was spoiled.

"They're here for babies too," Lucky said. "Most are with churches."

Emma twisted her napkin. "I can't wait to meet Xi'an Hua."

Lucky poured tea from a porcelain pot the color of moss. "Would you like to go shopping for souvenirs tomorrow?"

"This isn't a vacation." She apologized for snapping.

Sean and Lucky couldn't talk her into stopping off at the bar for a nightcap either. When she headed up to her room a young couple was already in the elevator. They were holding hands so tightly their fingers were white.

"Which floor?" the woman asked.

"Twenty-one," Emma said.

"The same as us." Her nose was raw and red either from the cold or crying. A gold cross on a gold chain gleamed below her throat. "What part of the States is home?"

"San Francisco."

"We're from South Bend. That's in Indiana. We're the Barkers. I'm Julie and this is my husband Jeff. Did you just arrive?" She spoke in a sing-song voice.

Emma nodded and watched the numbers blink.

"This is our fourth day. The Lord willing, we'll be holding our precious angel in our arms tomorrow. We've already picked out a name. Faith. Doesn't that say it all? Have you chosen one yet?"

"She already has a name. It's Xi'an Hua."

"Oh." Julie hesitated before starting up again. "Which church are you with? We're with Calvary Fellowship."

"I'm here with my brother."

"Wasn't your husband able to get time off work?"

"I'm a single mom." Emma said. "Well, I will be."

Julie's lips pursed before she said, "Remember, you're never alone. God is always with you."

Emma stabbed a floor button. The elevator lurched to a stop at 16.

"I thought you were staying on our floor?" Julie said.

"Good luck with your baby." Emma stepped out and ducked down the hall.

*

The next morning they took a taxi to the Children's Welfare Agency's offices. Emma was glad the car's ragged muffler drowned the sound of her beating heart. It sank when she entered the lobby. The air was ripe with anxiety and resignation like that of an airport terminal where half the flights have been canceled and the rest delayed. She pushed her way through the crowd and signed in at the front desk. Every chair was occupied so she joined Sean and Lucky who had found places to lean against the wall.

Lucky gave an impromptu lesson on Chinese insults. Sean's laughter at phrases like "stupid inbred stack of meat" and "you explosive water buffalo diarrhea" brought glares. Three hours passed before an unmarked door opened and a woman with steel gray hair and a suit the same color entered. Two younger women followed. They were dressed in silk blouses, tight jeans, and heels. The room grew silent as the older woman lifted a pair of silver wire-rimmed glasses that dangled from a chain. One of the younger women handed her a manila folder. She spent several minutes thumbing through it.

The woman pushed the glasses off her nose. The chain caught them as they fell. "I am Madame Sze. I have a list. I will read the list. When you hear your name, please form a line."

On cue, the young women swept their arms toward the unmarked door as if pointing to a prize curtain on a TV game show.

Madame Sze polished her glasses with a handkerchief before returning them to her nose.

Emma felt lightheaded until she realized she was holding her breath. She tried to remember the breathing exercises she'd learned in yoga. It had been a few weeks since she'd gone to class even though the studio was on the same floor as her workstation. Responsibility for launching an upgrade to the enterprise's bestselling app and planning for the trip to China had left her no time. The only way she'd been able to juggle both was by relying on the campus's onsite meals, laundry service, and hair salon.

"Simpkins, William and Leslie," Madame Sze said.

"Johnson, Richard and Barbara. Petrelli, Giancarlo and Eva."

Murmurs and moans followed as the couples formed a line. Someone started applauding, another cheered.

Madame Sze pushed the glasses off her nose. "All is complete."

She turned on her heel and marched toward the unmarked door. Her assistants shepherded the lucky couples to follow.

"That's it?" Emma said.

"Maybe she's gone to get another list," Lucky said. "I'll call my cousin."

Julie Baxter was sitting nearby. She leaned forward. "Now we have to wait until after lunch. She usually comes back in the afternoon with more names."

"I thought it would be more efficient, more organized," Emma said.

Julie leaned closer. "My husband says they do it on purpose to test us. Jeff and I have a little joke. Instead of naming our baby Faith, we're going to call her Patience."

Lucky called his cousin who confirmed the schedule. "We have time for lunch, Miss B. There's a place nearby that has the best walnut and sesame cakes in Nanchang."

Emma said she wasn't hungry. Sean looped his arm through hers. "Don't be so Joan of Arc. You have to keep your strength up. I hope they have beer."

*

Bowls and small plates clattered on trolleys pushed quickly between tables crowded with people chatting noisily on phones. Lucky made the selections.

"Okay, this one is egg and brown sauce, that's chicken with walnuts, and here's my all-time favorite Nanchang delicacy, flaky deep-fried beef balls. They don't have forks, is that okay?"

"We *are* from San Francisco, so we *do* know how to use chopsticks," Sean said.

"Here they're called *kuàizi*. Literal translation? Quick bamboo. Dig in."

Emma said, "Can your cousin do anything about setting up

a meeting with Madame Sze?"

"I can ask, but are you sure that's a good idea?"

"Why wouldn't it be? I want her to know I started the application process two years ago. If she knew that, maybe she won't make me wait any longer. The Barkers said they've been here four days and still haven't been called."

Lucky shrugged. "Maybe there's something wrong with their paperwork. Remember what I said about the bureaucracy here."

Sean made a moustache with his finger. "*Jawohl*, your papers, please."

While Sean and Lucky reeled off their favorite war movies, Emma picked at her food. Thinking there could be something wrong with her application knotted her stomach. What if she'd transposed a number or misspelled a word? What if her lawyer had forgotten to file something important? What if Xi'an Hua's birth parents had changed their minds?

Lucky pushed a plate of sliced cakes toward her. "Try one. They're made with sweet potato paste, green tea, and sesame seeds."

Emma took a nibble. "Delicious." Her tone said otherwise.

Lucky frowned before grinning. "You see everyone here on their phones? China's gone completely mobile. I'll bet you anything they use your app. How did you get into that line of work?"

"Like your name. Right place at the right time."

"But with Mr. Wrong," Sean added quickly.

Emma rolled her eyes. "A guy I was seeing was working at this little start-up. He got me a job there," she explained.

"Which happened to grow up to become a gazillion dollar company thanks to you and your obsession with work." Sean toasted her with a bottle of Snow beer and then gave Lucky his Jack Nicholson eyebrows imitation. "All work and no play makes Emma a dull girl."

"We should get back to the Agency," she said.

"See what I mean?" Sean said.

*

Emma sat in bed staring at her laptop. Before she left home she had scanned the photograph of Xi'an Hua from The Referral and made it her screen saver. That afternoon Madame Sze had called only two more couples. When she said "All is complete," Julie let out a sob. Emma instinctively reached over and patted her shoulder.

"Show me a picture of your baby," she said.

Julie sniffled and pulled a copy of The Referral from her purse. The photo was of a little girl about the same age as Xi'an Hua. She had chubby cheeks and a bit more hair. The tip of her tongue showed between her lips.

Emma read the name aloud. "Liling Lan. She's adorable."

Julie dabbed her eyes. "It's so hard to be patient sometimes. I want her so much."

"'Testing your faith produces endurance,'" her husband said. "James, Chapter 1, Verse 2."

"I'll try harder," she said.

Sitting up in bed, Emma whispered to the image on her computer screen. "Tomorrow, I promise."

She logged onto her company email. Her inbox showed over 200 unread messages that her assistant had culled from hundreds more. Emma read through the subject lines. It was as if the words were in a different language. She lowered the screen and set the device aside. As she rearranged the pillows and pulled the blankets up to her chin, she thought of what her brother had said about Mr. Wrong. Sean was right about him, but wrong about her not trying to have a relationship.

The problem was the men she met. There was the 40-something CEO who never outgrew wearing Star Trek T-shirts, the intellectual property attorney who could only talk about his own brilliance, the marketing consultant who neglected to mention his wife and kids back in New York. Her last attempt ended two years ago. She met him at a fundraiser for the hospital where Sean was completing his residency. For six months, she convinced herself he was the one until the night he told her she made him feel like one of his lung cancer patients. "I'm suffocating," he said. "If you want unconditional love so much, get a puppy."

As she tried to fall asleep, she vowed Xi'an Hua would never doubt she loved her no matter what.

*

The next two days were more of the same. Before and after lunch the hopeful parents-to-be would crowd into the lobby of the Agency and wait for Madame Sze to read out names. At the end of every appearance, she would utter the three words Emma feared hearing most: "All is complete." Every day a few people would leave with a child and more people would join the ranks of the hopeful. Emma vacillated between resenting and welcoming the newcomers as they were both competitors as well as evidence of advancement.

On the fourth day, Sean and Lucky didn't accompany her. Sean told her he was only a text message away and might as well get in some sightseeing since he was taking precious vacation time away from the hospital. Lucky excused himself by saying he could be more useful working the backchannels with his cousin.

Emma invited Julie Baxter to lunch when she learned the young woman's husband had gone to Beijing. When they were seated at the restaurant, she asked why he went.

"We need to get new visas," Julie said. "We've been here a year on a special missionary visa, but now they say we're in a different classification. I don't understand all the rules, but they're very strict about these sorts of things."

"Will you return to the U.S. when you get Liling Lan?"

"Who? Oh, you mean Faith. Yes. Jeff has a job waiting for him as a lay minister back in South Bend. I'll teach Sunday School."

"How long have you been married?"

"Three years last May." Julie's nose was rawer and redder than ever. Emma pictured her crying herself to sleep every night. "This will be the longest we've ever been apart."

"I'm sure he'll be back before you know it."

"God willing, the day after tomorrow."

"He couldn't get a better flight connection than that?"

Emma asked.

"He took the train. It's a lot less expensive."

"Do you mind if I ask how old you are?"

"I'm 22. And you?"

Emma paused. "Old enough to know better," she finally said.

"Oh," Julie said.

But when Emma smiled, Julie did too.

*

The bedside hotel phone startled her awake. The ring was unfamiliar and it took Emma a few moments to remember where she was. It was Julie calling.

"I've been throwing up all night." The young woman groaned.

"Do you want me to call my brother? He's a doctor."

"I'm sure it's something I ate. I've had it before. The village we lived in wasn't the cleanest."

"I feel terrible. It must have been the restaurant I took you too."

"It's not your fault, but could you do me a favor?"

"Of course."

"Jeff's not back and I don't feel well enough to go to the Agency this morning. I saw you have a cell phone. If Madame Sze calls our name, could you tell her I'll be right there and then call me here at the hotel?"

"Of course, but I'm sure they'd reschedule your appointment for the next day if I explained you're not feeling well and your husband had to go to Beijing."

"I don't want to risk it. We've waited so long. If they call our name, I'll get a taxi and come right over."

"If you're sure."

"I am. Thank you."

Before hanging up, Emma said, "Put the picture of your baby on your nightstand so you can look at her. That'll make you feel better. I'll ask Sean to check in on you."

"You're so nice."

Emma got up and opened the curtains. It was shortly past

dawn and the light was weak and the clouds dark. She put her hand on her stomach. It was tight from having eaten very little over the past few days, but if she had food poisoning too, she'd already be sick by now. She decided to skip breakfast anyway. Not even a cup of tea.

*

She was first in line at the Agency that morning and got a seat. The room filled and the low murmur of voices soothed rather than irritated her as it usually did. She closed her eyes and settled in for another long day. Her thoughts drifted. Growing up near Golden Gate Park. Going on summer vacations to Lake Tahoe. Sean coming into her bedroom one night and crying that his boyfriend had dumped him. She telling him, he'd get over it. He hunching his back and mimicking Charles Laughton: "Why was I not made of stone like thee?"

Emma barely registered the bustle of the unmarked door opening and Madame Sze and her two assistants marching into the lobby. The instructions were given about lining up, the silver wire rimmed glasses polished, the manila folder passed, and the lucky winners announced.

"Wachowsky, Bert and Elizabeth. Hagensen, Olav and Liv. Baxter, Jeffrey and Julie. Burke, Emma." Madame Sze pushed the glasses off her nose. "All is complete."

Emma blinked. Had she heard correctly? Had Madame Sze finally called her name? Did she also say Julie? The line was already forming. An assistant held the door open.

"Wait," Emma shouted as she hurried after them. "Wait, I'm Burke, Emma."

Madame Sze didn't break stride. The other assistant gestured for Emma to fall in at the end of the line.

"Did she also call Baxter?" Emma asked her. "Jeff and Julie?"

The assistant's smile was frozen. "Please," and swung her arms toward the open door.

It led to a hallway lined with more doors. Each was numbered. The assistants called names and pointed to doors. Emma was ushered into Room 3. She tried to remember if the number was considered lucky by the Chinese. A pair of chairs in front of a metal desk and a chair behind were the only furnishings. She decided not to call Julie until she could ask about the possibility of rescheduling.

The door to Room 3 opened and a middle-aged man dressed in a baggy suit the same color as Madame Sze's entered. He nodded to her and sat behind the desk. Emma pulled her file from her handbag and placed it in front of her. She didn't wait for him to begin.

"Good morning, I'm Emma Burke. I love Xi'an Hua. I promise I'll be the best mother ever. Here is my file."

The man made no move to take it. "I am Mr. Fong. Please to accept our apology."

Emma nodded as she opened her folder and fanned the pages. "Here's my application, my letters of reference, medical records, correspondence between the agencies, and, of course, The Referral. What else do you need to know about me? Ask any question you want. When can I meet Xi'an Hua?"

"Your file is most complete, Miss Burke. However, please to accept our apology. There is a most regrettable situation."

"What do you mean, *situation*?"

"Please to understand these things happen. There has been a change."

"What kind of change?"

"Regrettably, the child is no longer available."

The room spun. Emma gripped the table to try and slow it down. "Is this because I'm single?" She pushed the folder toward him. "Please read my file. Xi'an Hua will want for nothing. Ever. She'll have the best home, live in the best neighborhood, go to the best schools, and receive the finest medical care. My brother is a doctor. He'll be like a father to her. My parents will be devoted grandparents. Xi'an Hua will be loved and taken care of. I promise you."

"Please, Miss Burke."

"Is it about money? Are there more fees, another permit I need to pay? Fine. Tell me how much."

Mr. Fong waved his hands. "No, no. Please to understand.

The child is no longer available."

Emma grabbed The Referral and held it up. She pointed at the photograph. "Of course she's available. Look at the date. All the official red stamps. See, her picture is right here. Right on The Referral. Xi'an Hua. Xi'an Hua. See, that's her name. It's written right here."

Mr. Fong folded his hands and bowed. "There is no longer a record for this child. It is most rare. Perhaps there was a clerical error. Perhaps her family reclaimed her. Perhaps she took ill."

Emma clasped her chest. Her breath came in gasps and she hiccupped as she struggled to speak. "Are you telling me she's dead?"

"Please to understand. There is no longer a record. You must resubmit your application and receive a new Referral. Regrettably, this will take additional time, but please to be patient."

Emma leapt up and smacked the desk. "No. I won't wait another minute. I want to see Madame Sze. Right now." She held up her phone. "Did you see my letters of reference? One is from a member of the U.S. Congress. One is from the CEO of my company. He used to work at the White House. One call. That's all it will take to make this turn into something you don't want. Go get Madame Sze. I need to see her now." She smacked the desk again. "Right now."

Fong hurried from the room. Emma collapsed back in the chair. She called Lucky. He answered on the second ring.

"What's up, Miss B?"

"I need you and your cousin at the Agency right away. They're trying to pull some bullshit about my baby. Hurry."

"Did you speak to Madame Sze?"

"I'm waiting for her now. I told the man who said I can't have Xi'an Hua to go get her."

"What man?"

"Some man who works here. He said his name is Fong."

"Oh no, Miss B. Fong is my cousin."

Emma hung up and buried her face in the crook of her

arm. She breathed in, breathed out. She kept at it and lost track of time. The door finally opened and Madame Sze entered. She took the seat across from Emma and placed a manila folder in front of her. They stared wordlessly at each other for what seemed like minutes. The older woman's lips were an irritated crease and her pupils shined like black cherries behind the silver wire rimmed glasses. Finally, she opened the folder and scanned several pages as she turned them. Then she closed it and pushed the glasses from the bridge of her nose and the silver chain arrested their fall.

She crooked her finger at Emma. "The Referral."

Emma held onto it. She kept her stare fixed on the older woman. "I want my child. I need her here now."

Madame Sze did not blink. "The Referral," she said again.

Emma relented. Madame Sze did not put her glasses back on or read it. She tucked it beneath the stack of papers in her folder and then took the top sheet and slid it to Emma.

"All is complete."

Emma read it. It was a Referral like the one she'd handed Madame Sze only with the day's date. The ink of the official red stamps looked wet. The photograph at the bottom was of a girl with chubbier cheeks and a bit more hair than Xi'an Hua. The tip of her tongue stuck between her lips as if she were nursing. Emma took a deep breath before reading the name. Liling Lan.

"But Julie Barker," she said.

"You are not Burke, Emma?" Madame Sze challenged.

"I am, but…" Emma pointed at the photo. "This isn't the right child."

"A child is neither right nor wrong. It is a child."

Madame Sze stood. "You want child, return at four pm sharp. All is complete."

*

Emma clutched her phone as she walked out of the Agency. The sky was dull as lead. Raindrops stung like pellets shot from a gun. She ignored the taxis out front and started to run. She ignored the downpour, the puddles, the sloshing in her shoes.

She kept on running.

Tendrils of hair stuck to her face, but Emma didn't bother to push them away. She hurried past an ancient temple with turned-up eaves that resembled the prows of boats surging up the face of a storm-lashed wave. Yellow banners streamed from the rafters. An enormous pair of wooden doors beckoned at the end of a cloistered courtyard paved in stone. Emma hesitated and then turned toward them. She passed between statues of a lion and dragon that guarded the front steps. Intricate carvings of elephants, monkeys, lions, and gourds graced the doors. Their handles depicted a tortoise intertwined with a serpent.

The only light inside the sanctuary came from candles flickering on a gold altar that held baskets of fruit and bowls of water. The air was thick with the smell of jasmine and orange blossoms. Emma could see murals of people planting, fishing, and tending animals on the walls. She could tell the floor was made of wood by the way it creaked.

Sticks of incense bristled from large bronze pots placed on either side of the altar. Their tips glowed red while snakeskins of white ash slithered around their trunks. Emma shivered, not from the damp and cold, but from the realization that so many things were beyond her ken, so much beyond her control.

A monk cloaked in a brown robe stepped from the shadows. He was hairless except for eyelashes the color of incense ash. He put his fingertips together in the shape of a steeple and touched it to his forehead.

"I'm sorry, I don't speak Chinese," Emma said. "I hope I'm not trespassing, but I was passing by and something drew me here."

The monk bowed.

"You probably can't understand what I'm saying," she said, hurrying her words. "I need help. I have to make a decision and don't know what to do."

The monk reached out and touched her forehead. He uttered something and then approached the nearest pot of incense. He bowed to it and then pulled a square of paper from his robe, folded it in half, and then in half again. He held an edge against a glowing ember. When the paper ignited, he cupped it in his hands. He did not seem to feel the flame as he held it out so the smoke could mingle with that of the incense. When the paper had been consumed, he rubbed the ashes between his palms and then blew the gray powder toward the altar.

The monk bowed to Emma. "Release of spirit," he said, his English soft and low. "Spirit now on Tao path."

He shuffled away on straw sandals without looking back.

Emma stared into the glow of the temple's candles and saw the past two years rush toward her. All of the effort, the frustrations, the agonizing over whether or not she could truly open herself to someone else struck her. And struck hard. She wobbled. She was cold, she was hungry, and she was tired. So very tired.

Water dripping from clothes drummed on the wooden floor like a steady heartbeat. The sound brought Emma back to the moment. She reached into her bag and plucked a copy of the photo of Xi'an Hua. She kissed it and then folded it into a tiny square. She touched an edge to the glowing ember at the tip of a stick of incense. When the folded paper ignited, she cupped the flame in her hands and bit her lip to keep from crying out. And when it had turned to ash, she rubbed her palms together and blew the powder away.

*

The flight attendant grew tired of filling Sean's glass, so she wrapped a bottle of champagne in a white cloth and placed it on his tray table.

"Thanks," Sean told her. He toasted Emma. "And thank you for the upgrade. I could get used to first class."

"The least I could do," she said.

"I'll say. You owe me big time." He said it with a grin, but when she didn't reply, he softened. "You okay?"

"It's been a long week."

"No kidding." He gave an exaggerated yawn. "Who would have thought it'd go the way it did?"

"Life is unpredictable."

"I always knew my big sister was tough, but putting up with everything and then have them pull the rug out." He feigned a shiver.

Emma reclined her seat. Maybe she'd finally be able to fall asleep.

Sean leaned across the aisle. "Don't beat yourself up. Regrets and guilt are part of life."

"I know."

And she thought about all the things that had run through her mind when she was at the temple. How unfair it all was. How a one-child mandate and an overburdened orphanage system forced to deal with it was to blame. How it wasn't Jeff's fault he had to go to Beijing or Julie's for getting sick. How if the Agency could swap Liling Lan for Xi'an Hua, then there was no guarantee it wouldn't assign her to someone else.

In the end, Emma realized none of that mattered because Madame Sze's test for her had never been about patience and faith. She glanced down at the lie-flat seat between hers and the window. Liling Lan was asleep on her side, her cheek rising and falling, the tip of her tongue pink like a kitten's. The child was proof that Emma had what it took.

She turned to Sean. "I hope Julie can…"

He cut her off with a wave of his glass, screwed up his face, and adopted one of his movie voices. "Forget it, Emma; it's Chinatown."

NATURAL SELECTION

When you're a Darwin and your parents name you Charles, they put a lot of expectations on you right from the get-go. Like, you're supposed to do something bigger than sail around on a boat named for a dog and study birds and lizards. Third smartest thing I ever did? Calling myself Charlie instead of Charles. Chuck wasn't an option because of that ancient song "The Name Game." *Shirley! Shirley, Shirley Bo-bir-ley, bo-na-na fanna Fo-fir-ley, fee fi Mo-mir-ley, Shirley!* I figured I could live with Bo-bar-lie, bo-na-na fanna fo-far-lie, but Chuck? No way.

Second smartest thing I ever did? Walked into the career office the semester I tried City College and spotted a posting for a job at the zoo. It's the only time my name paid off. The lady in charge of hiring said it must be fate. I started on April first, and they put me to work answering phones in the front office. Kids called all day long. Some adults too. "Is a Mr. Lyon there? No? April Fools!" Part of the job was keeping a tally of all the different names. Mrs. Ella Fant and Mr. G. Raff ran neck and neck for top of the list. My vote for cleverest? Miss Ranga Tang.

Office work wasn't for me, so I asked to work the cages. We're supposed to call them homes in front of the visitors. That or natural habitats. I started off shoveling shit and hosing down floors and walls. Baboons were the worst. And not because the males run around with hard-ons and hump everything in sight. Why the keepers give them names like Rodney, Peterbuilt, and Congressman Boehner. No, it's because they pick up their own shit and throw it all over the place. See who can chuck it the farthest or make the best graffiti.

I still push a shovel all right, but I worked my way up, starting with helping corral the muskox when they needed their hooves checked—did you know the fronts are bigger than the backs?—to brushing a hippo's teeth; I used a push broom. I also got shifts walking around the zoo holding a koala or a boa draped around my neck. In two seconds, I'd get a crowd around me asking questions and wanting to pet it. Young mothers pushing babies in strollers, packs of cute teenyboppers taking selfies with me and whatever I'm holding, dudes all tatted up trying to act tough in front of their girlfriends who wear high heels to the zoo. "Hey man, that little bear bite? You don't worry about the snake choking you? How often that bird shit on your shoulder?"

Some of the other keepers call me Dr. Doolittle. And it's not because I enjoy my breaks as much as the next guy or take the occasional siesta in the shed where we store hay for the camels. It's because I got a special way with animals. Not all, but some. Mainly the ones been here the longest. I take one look at the old zebra and know she's going to go off her feed because her saliva dried up again. Or when the silverback is in one of his moods, so I don't put the juveniles in with him even though the enclosure—sorry, natural habitat—is an entire acre. He gets to chasing them around and yelling at them, it scares the visitors half to death.

It was one of the reasons why the new vet took to asking me to assist a lot more often than the old vet ever did. He was all up in himself and treated keepers like second-class citizens, barking orders and calling us janitors, but Dr. Laurie? She was the exact opposite. Super sweet and super smart. Super good looking too and always quick with a smile. I figured she was way out of my league, for sure, but I liked it when she started giving a call for help. I even programmed my zoo phone with a special ringtone for her—a female cheetah; cheetah's chirp, don't roar—so I knew to drop whatever I was doing and go running.

First time I helped her was when a flamingo split his bill. Big crack in it, so when he tried to suck up brine it all squirted out. I waded right into the pond with a net and all the flamingos went nuts. It was like a pink tornado swirling around and making a racket you wouldn't believe. Honking, clucking, squealing. Dr. Laurie was watching, so I played it cool and professional and singled out the hurt bird and bagged him on the first try without ruffling a feather. I carried him into the operating room and said, "What are you going to do, superglue it back together?" And she flashed that smile of hers and said, "Exactly." So I cradled the bird and held his head steady while she glued both sides of the crack in his bill and then blew it with a hairdryer. Afterwards, she said I got hands as steady as a surgeon's.

Best time I ever helped her was when Frosty got pregnant. Frosty is a polar bear whose real name is Tlun, which is Eskimo for snow that sparkles with moonlight. They got 50 different words for snow, but all the kids call her Frosty even though she's not a snowman. Most of the keepers don't like Frosty because she can be pretty ornery. I tell them, what do you expect? Even though it's always cold and foggy out by the zoo, San Francisco's not the North Pole. Not by a longshot.

Frosty got artificially knocked up as part of a plan to save polar bears because ice is melting all over the place. One day, Dr. Laurie asked if I could work graveyard because according to the calendar, Frosty was due to have her baby. I said no problem, and not because it meant overtime, but because whatever she wanted I couldn't said no. I figured the job was to babysit Frosty and if it looked like she was about to pop, call Dr. Laurie. But when I showed up at Frosty's indoor cage to stand watch, there was Dr. Laurie with a thermos of coffee, sandwiches, and two chairs from the front office.

We sat there talking and watching Frosty like we were sitting at home in front of the TV. It was nice. She told me her life story, how she always loved animals, how she went to vet school at Davis and got her degree, worked at an elephant orphanage in Africa for a while, and then married some guy who was over there on safari. He was a banker or some kind of financial genius, I forget which. Best of all, she told me she wanted to work at the zoo for the rest of her life. Me too, I told her.

Then she asked about me, and so I went right in with the name thing, and she even remembered the song even though it was written like a hundred years before she was born and said she understood my point. Said it without laughing. She asked if the real Charles Darwin was a relative. I told her maybe because my old man is originally from England, but his name is Leslie, which is a regular name for a dude over there, but here in San Francisco he goes with plain Les on account the regulars he pours for at the Drum and Major are phobic everything, not that I spend much time there. It's filled with dudes my old man's age who are more Rooney than Beckham. And that's just for starters. Women hardly go there at all. They like the Irish bars where there's music and dancing. Cheaper drinks, more laughter, and plenty of firemen still wearing their blues.

Dr. Laurie said, "Is that where you go, to Irish bars?" And I told her, "Yeah, O'Malley's after work because it's close." And she gave that laugh of hers and said, "And I bet you don't change out of your uniform beforehand either."

How she knew that, I don't know, but it's true. There's something about that zoo patch embroidered above the heart of my khaki shirt. When women see it they go all, ooh, I love baby animals. I didn't tell Dr. Laurie this part, but plenty of times after a couple of drinks they ask if I can sneak them into the zoo right then and there. Sure, I say, knowing exactly how it's going to go.

The first time, the woman asks to see the lions. The pride sleeps inside at night, so I take her there and the male wakes up and stares at us through the wire. Then he jumps up and stalks back and forth and shakes his head and bares his teeth. The woman gets scared and grabs hold of me. The next thing I know we're doing it on the floor right in front of the cage. "Roar," she tells me. "Roar like a lion." Okay, what the heck, so I do. She left scratches on my back. Another time, this woman asks me to take her to see the gorillas. The silverback sleeps alone behind a thick glass wall, not wire, because you don't want a gorilla who can snap a tree trunk to be able to stick his hands out. As soon as we get there, she does a striptease in front of him. That wakes him up, all right. Then she pushes me up against the glass, and we do it standing up with him just on the other side. No way I was ever going to tell Dr. Laurie about that.

Anyway, Dr. Laurie and me, we finished the sandwiches and were sipping coffee when Frosty started going around in circles and laying down and getting back up and so on. "This is it," she said. And sure enough, about an hour later out came a little cub. It was about the size of a white rat only without the tail. Seeing that big old momma bear that everyone thinks is so mean treat that tiny little baby so gently, well, I got a tear in my eye, for sure. Dr. Laurie looked over at me, and so did she.

Morning rolled around and she asked me to distract Frosty with a piece of seal meat so she could sneak in and check over the baby and weigh it and take a blood sample and everything. I told her I didn't think it was such a good idea, knowing Frosty's temper, but Dr. Laurie said it would be just fine. And it was. So, along with super smart and super good looking, add super brave. The zoo held a naming contest for the baby polar bear, which Dr. Laurie determined was a boy, and we got more entries than we do phone calls on April Fool's Day. The winner was Tlatim, which means little snowflake in Eskimo, but everyone called him Jon Snow because of *Game of Thrones*.

That night watching Frosty give birth was Dr. Laurie's and my little secret. I'd swing by the bears' home every chance I got because just looking at the mom and cub, which was growing like crazy, made me remember how special that night was. And when my zoo phone gave the cheetah chirp, I'd run even faster, thinking about the birth, even though no job with Dr. Laurie afterward was near as fun. Like, pulling a splinter out of a mandrill's butt or cleaning mites from a meerkat's ears.

A couple of months went by and I started noticing a change in Dr. Laurie. Her smile didn't turn on as quick and she sort of lost her usual glow. I asked her if everything was all right one time when I was holding a hundred-year-old tortoise for her while she checked his temperature, but she shrugged and said she was just tired is all. I let it go, it wasn't my place to dig, and then I didn't see her for a couple of weeks or so. The lady in the front office said she was taking some personal time.

Then one night I stopped off at O'Malleys on my way home and there she was sitting at the bar. There was a fireman on either side chatting her up and when I go over to say hello, I saw she's working on an Irish Car Bomb and the way she's talking I knew it wasn't her first. The firemen gave me looks that said, "Hey, pal, you don't got a chance here. We're June and July. Have you looked in the mirror lately?" But they didn't know what I knew.

I said to Dr. Laurie, "Hey, Frosty and Jon Snow sure do miss you." It was like the firemen suddenly went up in smoke and it was just the two of us alone. Patrick brought me over my regular—a cream ale with a whisky back—and Dr. Laurie and me clinked glasses for the first time since I'd known her. I took my time asking her where she'd been and what she was doing here, never having seen her at O'Malley's before but remembering how I mentioned it to her the night we watched Frosty give birth.

We beat around it for a while. I told her the substitute vet they brought in didn't hold a candle to her, that a chimp escaped Monkey Island and I found it taking a crap beneath the zoo director's desk, and how the male Greater Kudu got his horns stuck in the fence. And then I dropped it in, casual like, and asked her what was new with her. But instead of answering, she grabbed my hand and said, "Let's go to the zoo, Charlie. Let's go right now."

She looped her arm through mine as we made the walk over and I told myself it was because the fog was swirling pretty thick and she'd downed all those Car Bombs, which can make even the biggest, strongest fireman stagger. No way I was going to let myself think about how I'd made the same walk with those other women before.

I gave the night watchman the high sign when we got there, and he unlocked the gate before I even got my keys out and said, "Welcome back, Dr. Laurie." I told him we were checking on a patient and he said, "Of course you are."

We headed toward the animal hospital, but then she said, "Let's go see the tigers." I got to admit, I never got the words *are you sure* out.

Like all the zoo's big cats, the tigers were in their sleeping pens for the night. As we stood there looking at them, Dr. Laurie let it all out. How her husband got this big job offer in New York City and decided to take it. How she told him that would mean she'd have to give up her job and she didn't want to. How he told her she could find one back there because there were, like, five different zoos. How she agreed to go and see, but there weren't any openings. How when she told him, he said she didn't need to work anyway, that he was making plenty of money, and if she wanted to keep busy, well, she could always get a job taking care of rich people's poodles.

"So we split up," she said. "And here I am."

I said her husband wasn't such a big shot after all, just a big shithead. And she looped her arm back through mine and squeezed. We watched the sleeping tigers for a while longer, and then she asked if I knew a guy named Frank Stockton. I said no, but I wondered if maybe he was one of the firemen at O'Malley's.

"He's a writer who wrote a short story called "The Lady, or the Tiger?" she said.

I said I'd never read it, so she told it to me. It wasn't about a zoo at all, but about this king who makes dudes accused of a crime choose between two doors. Behind one is a beautiful lady and the other a tiger. If he guesses right, he's declared innocent and gets to marry the girl. If he chooses wrong, he's declared guilty and gets eaten. One day, the king finds out some dude is sleeping with his daughter, so he puts him to the test. The daughter finds out the girl behind the door is her rival so when her boyfriend looks at her for help in choosing doors, she points to one. He goes to open it, but the story ends before you know which one she told him to pick. I don't like stories that don't have an ending where the good guy wins and the bad guy gets it, but I don't say that to Dr. Laurie. I just told her it was pretty interesting to leave you guessing like that.

After a long pause, she said, "I suppose that's what I did. I chose to make my husband choose between his job and me."

I can't remember the exact words I said because it gets all kind of garbled up when I'm trying to explain stuff, but it was something like she made the right choice to see where he stood and he made the wrong choice telling her where he stood. And she squeezed my arm again and said, "That's what I love about you, Charlie. I know I can always count on you." I didn't know what to say after hearing that, but it made me feel pretty good.

The big male tiger, Raj, finally woke up and eyed us. His tail started twitching back and forth. Dr. Laurie tightened her grip on my arm and I started thinking, I can't believe this is going to happen. And then she said, "If there were two closed doors and it was like the story, and I was behind one and Raj behind the other, would you risk choosing if you could have me?"

The way she said it, I knew there was a whole lot of Irish Car Bombs talking there. I mean, you drop a shot of Bailey's in a pint of Guinness and chug it, and do that two or three times, you're likely to say or do anything. So I gave it some thought and said—and here's where those shots of Jameson I'd done myself were helping form the words—"Wild animals couldn't stop me."

"You really would risk life and death for me, wouldn't you?" she said, all serious, and leaning against me like we were sharing my jacket.

"I would," I said, not telling her that Raj and me go way back, long before she became the vet. I'm the only keeper at the zoo he lets come into his sleeping pen without making so much as a growl. He all but purrs for me. It's that Dr. Doolittle thing I got.

Dr. Laurie leaned in even closer and stuck her lips right against my ear. "You don't have to choose a door, Charlie. I'm right here, right now."

First smartest thing I ever did? Deciding right then and there that if I went ahead with it, I might as well be killed by a tiger because the next day what we had between us would be deader than a doornail. No way I wanted to risk losing that.

So I told her I had a better idea, that we should go over and pull a couple of chairs in front of Frosty and Jon Snow's and watch them sleep and in the morning I'd help her with the new bongo that had arrived when she was gone. A wildebeest kicked him in the shin and the wound looked like it was getting infected. And so that's what we did.

BETWEEN WIND AND WATER

Leo stepped out of the tin-roofed sugar shack to the sound of bells and chickens. A dozen churches tended to the spiritual needs of 'Ōlauniu, one for every hundred people. Not that everyone went to church and not that those who did went to only one. Attendance varied depending on which church was featuring which musician or holding a luau. Most of the preachers in the old plantation town on the Big Island took an aloha view when it came to competing for souls. They even agreed to stagger services and the bells. The first to ring was Our Lady of Perpetua followed by Akua Hale Baptist, Palms Methodist, Kahu Congregational, and Hongjanwi Buddhist. The Latter Day Saints temple didn't have chimes, nor did the meeting halls for the Adventists and Witnesses; they also weren't big on hosting slack key guitarists who played reggae instead of traditional.

The rooster crowed before them all. It had crowed at the break of day every day since Leo moved in, and it crowed every night, all through the night, because it kept tripping a motion-activated floodlight in his neighbor's garden. The light show and cock-a-doodle-doing made a full night's sleep impossible, and insomnia was taking its toll. Working on a 30-story tower perched on the edge of the pali required a clear mind, not to mention nerves of steel and an iron grip.

Leo had structured his life to minimize social interaction, but there was no choice but to suck it up and see if he could convince his neighbor to kill the light or the rooster. He walked across the field. Two untethered goats and a horse kept it from becoming jungle. The neighbor's place was identical to his own, right down to the rust-stained roof, faded green siding, and sagging lanai. Both once housed field hands before the sugar cane industry went bust.

The open front door stopped him short. "Hello," he called. "Anyone home?"

A woman with black hair streaked with gray and tattooed armbands appeared. She tilted her head and gave a wry smile. "Finally you find your way over. It so far you got lost before?"

"Sorry, I've been meaning to introduce myself, but work got in the way."

"Mo' bettah you get out of its way."

"I'm Leo, and I'm staying at Mr. Daijo's place."

"Mr.?" When she laughed her teeth flashed like breaking waves. "You talking about Larry D who probably charging you too much for that shack in the first place. Don't give him a bigger head than he already got since he started managing the Jade Empress. You smart to move out of there."

"How did you know I was staying at the hotel?"

"'Ōlauniu not so big not everybody not know everything. You the wind man. When we going get cheap electricity like we was promised, eh?"

"Pretty soon," he said.

She leaned toward him. He smelled coconut. "How soon?"

Leo remembered the public relations training about making promises. "I can have someone from Hawaii Electric call you. They can answer any questions you have. I work for the company that installed the turbine, so I only know about the operations side of the project."

Surf crested again. "I'm only having fun with you. I went to the meetings at the community hall. 'Clean and green,' they say, like Hawai'i not that already. I'm Liliko'i. Same as the fruit, only sweeter. Call me Lili. Everybody does. You want some breakfast, eh? I got fresh eggs and papaya too. That is unless you late for church."

"No, I'm not late." He stopped before saying he'd never been to church, not unless he counted the outdoor rock festivals his parents dragged him and his sister to when they lived in a converted school bus. "Actually, it's your chickens I wanted to talk to you about. The rooster mainly."

"Ah, King Kamehameha. Handsome, eh? Royal from his red crown and golden breast down to tip of his emerald tail. You see how he shines? Like a jewel."

"Yeah, he's pretty all right, but he's also pretty noisy. At night, I mean. Every time he triggers your garden light, he thinks it's sunup and starts crowing."

Her tattoos flexed when she crossed her arms. "I only hear him when he wakes me up in the morning like he supposed to."

"The truth is, I'm losing sleep because of him."

"Hmm. Where you from, Leo? The mainland?"

"California."

"You live in a big town over there?"

"I travel a lot for work, but the company is based in San Francisco."

"I been there. My niece married a Tongan who works at the airport. Big wedding. Lots of good food. Too cold for me though. All that fog." She mimed shuddering. "I like Vegas. It nice and warm. The aunties and me go there when the airline has special discount flight." She looked around before lowering her voice. "I do pretty good at blackjack. I count cards."

"Look, about the chicken, the rooster. Can you turn your garden light off?"

"Only if you want to spend the night in there keeping out pigs and dogs. Pig make a bigger mess than ten people with hoes who don't know nothing about hoeing. They only good for eating, especially kālua pig slow-cooked in imu." She made a mmm mmm good sound. "If a dog kills my hens, then there won't be no eggs. And if there no eggs, there no shells for compost, and then no vegetables. You the wind man, you know how it works." She drew a circle with her finger and winked. "Sustainable, eh?"

Lili pushed her hair back. She wore red coral rings that matched a necklace. "You married, Leo?"

"No."

"Got a partner?"

He shook his head.

"That what I thought. You staying at the Jade Empress all by yourself and now moved over here all alone. See, if you had someone to sleep with, you wouldn't be staying awake listening to King Kamehameha all night long."

"Yeah, but… "

"How about a phone? You got a phone?"

He nodded.

"You like our music?"

"Sure, but… "

"Tell you what you do. You don't bring headphones with you, you go over to Hasegawa Mercantile and buy a pair. Make sure to ask for Kama'aina discount. Then when you go to bed at night, you put on some Izzy. He the best. You sleep like a baby. Problem solved."

"Thanks for the tip."

Lili grinned. "What are neighbors for, eh? You want to come in and have a plate now? I'll make eggs and Spam and tell you about my daughter Makani. She not here right now, but you two should meet. You got plenty in common."

*

Leo's job was to make sure a wind power system was running according to specs after a construction crew had completed the install. It was always a race against time because profit margins were thin and overruns costly. After several years with the company, he'd earned a reputation as a troubleshooter who could be counted on to complete a project on time and under budget no matter how remote the location, how pesky the bugs in the software that controlled everything from monitoring the speed of the turbine to changing the yaw of the blades to deciding how much juice to send to the grid.

Leo took pride in his ability to tame something as wild as the wind. The fact that it required nonstop travel was a bonus. Growing up with parents whose idea of putting down roots was planting marijuana in national forests and then splitting right after harvest or when they got tipped a ranger was about to bust them had never instilled much of a sense of home or place. He didn't go to a school with walls until his first day of college. The title of his personal essay was "I Know Why the Caged 1968 Blue Bird Sings." It won him a scholarship to the University of California Santa Cruz, but classrooms did little to ground him. He transferred to three different UC campuses and spent a semester abroad two years out of four before graduating.

He'd been given one month to fine tune the wind machine at 'Ōlauniu so it would pass inspection. But the deadline was approaching fast. Though it was only a single tower, its problems were compounded by location. Hawai'i's northern tip was battered by capricious winds, so many different kinds that each had a name, like it was a person. Ahiaku, 'Āpa'apa'a, Kipu, Moa'e, and Pu'ukōlea. They ranged in power, from a gentle breeze called Kaiāulu to 'Ōlauniu, a blast that could shred a palm frond.

Leo had spelled the names with diacritical marks the way the locals pronounced them in a progress report he sent to the home office to explain what he was up against. It earned an instant retort from his supervisor: "Christ, Leo, don't go all native on me. Wind's wind the same as a fart's a fart. Just fix it and do it fast. Construction on the New Mexico project is nearly finished. I needed you there yesterday."

A breakthrough came when Leo completed sorting out the wiring on the main distribution panel—he'd grown convinced it had been assembled by someone with colorblindness since all the leads were reversed. Next up was tracking down a glitch with the anemometer that was sending faulty information to the controller and causing it to keep switching between the high- and low-speed shafts. Without a fix, the gearbox and generator would burn out.

Leo waited for a cloudless sky and gentle breeze before climbing the 300-rung ladder inside the hollow tower so he could get to the high-tech whirligig. It was attached to the rear of the turbine. When he reached the top of the ladder, he opened a hatch and climbed on top of the nacelle that housed the turbine. From his perch, he could see Maui across the channel. A pod of humpback whales had gathered between the two islands to breed. Some were spyhopping to look for mates, others were slapping the water with their tails to signal their whereabouts. A silvery ribbon of a waterfall to the west shimmered as it spilled down the face of a thousand-foot-high pali. Waves bulged one after another over a reef and raced to break on a black sand beach.

He didn't waste any time appreciating the view, but instead went straight to work. He examined the anemometer and checked its spinning cups and tail. All appeared intact. He unscrewed the base plate so he could check the signal wires for a faulty connection. As he did, a cloud drifted in front of the sun. He paid no attention to the shadow. The breeze picked up and the cloud split like an amoeba. Then the pair split and split again. A light rain began to fall. Leo was used to the warm and gentle tropical showers that came and went, but the breeze was becoming a steady gust and the sprinkles rain. He quickly replaced the protective base plate to protect the wiring. Before he could finish and climb back down the interior ladder, thunder boomed and lightning veined the darkening sky. The clouds let loose. Rain pelted Leo's face. Wind plucked at his shirt. The tower swayed. As he hung on tight and rode it out, he pictured himself as a sailor lashed to the mast of a bucking schooner.

Eventually, the squall blew itself out. The clouds parted and the sun reappeared. A rainbow arched overhead and the spouts of the humpbacks resembled plumeria blossoms. As Leo wiped the rain from his face, he realized no one would ever know what he'd just experienced.

*

A few days later his sister called. Seeing her name on the display surprised him since they hadn't spoken for months.

"What part of the world are you in?" Aries asked.

"Hawaii," he said.

"It must be beautiful there. Peaceful too."

"Not if you count the rooster next door. He's made it his personal business to keep me from sleeping."

Aries sighed. "I didn't track you down halfway around the world to hear you complain about some chicken."

"What's wrong?"

"It's Pine and Luna. They've finally gone and done it this time."

Their parents taught Aries and Leo to call them by their totem names. Their explanation was the children's true mother was Earth and their father the sun. When Leo was considering college in hopes it would give him a ticket off the bus, he told his parents he would have to list their given names on the application. They stroked each other's hands and gazed into each other's eyes. "The day has finally come," Pine said. And then they looked skyward and chanted together, "Your star child is ready to launch. Watch him shine as he blazes across the universe."

"Don't tell me they got busted again," Leo said.

"No, it's nothing like that." Aries took a deep breath. "They sold the bus to some rich guy from Silicon Valley for his personal car museum. He paid them a fortune. They bought a piece of land up in Humboldt and are growing acres of pot. They got one of those medical licenses. Pine bought a really expensive four-wheel-drive truck. He even started carrying an iPhone. And Luna? You wouldn't believe it. She goes to a nail salon now."

"Well, at least I won't have to send them money anymore."

"It's not funny. Don't you see? They've turned everything upside down. The Blue Bird was our home. And our parents? It's like I don't even know them."

"You should be relieved. They're not getting any younger. And neither was the bus."

"I'm serious. I'm very upset." Her voice started quavering. "I thought I could always count on them being there for me."

"As long as you could find out where they were parked."

"Don't be so mean."

Leo switched to deflection. "How's Roger and the kids?"

Aries sighed. "Oh, fine, I guess. Rog got a promotion and Janey and Billy are both playing soccer."

"Give them my best. Hey, I got to run."

"You're always running off. Where are you going next?"

"New Mexico as soon as I finish up here."

"Why don't you spend Christmas with us?"

"I'll have to see."

"Wait a sec, guess who I ran into the other day? Sondra Ricklefs. She asked about you. I always liked her. You two had a good thing going until you blew it. She still calls you Perry Grination, but not in a good way."

"I'll give you a call when I get there. New Mexico, that is."

*

The Jade Empress stood in the middle of a block in what passed for downtown 'Ōlauniu. The two-story hotel was built in the 1920s, and little had been done in the way of updating beyond new paint and bedding in its dozen guestrooms. The restaurant was popular with tourists and locals alike. Leo had eaten all his meals there when he was staying at the hotel, but now that he was trying to save money, he cooked for himself on a hotplate at the sugar shack. The one exception was Friday night when the Jade Empress offered a special menu and well drinks for half price.

Larry Daijo was behind the bar instead of the usual bartender. "What happened to Steve?" Leo asked.

"Howzit brah? He go to O'ahu for a wedding or funeral, I don' remember which, but a lot of time, they da same."

Leo sat on a stool. "You didn't tell me about the chicken next door."

"What chicken?"

"The neighbor's rooster. King Kamehameha. He crows all night long."

Larry D was wiry and his goatee wispy. "Don' know about no crowin', brah."

"Lili told me you tried to buy him because you thought he'd make a good fighter."

Larry D's eyebrows were wispy too. The hairs moved like

spider legs when he scrunched his forehead. "Cockfightin' against da law, brah. Everybody know dat."

Leo ordered a beer. Larry D said, "What wrong with crowin' anyway? It island music. You go to Kaua'i, there wild chickens by da thousands. They got loose from Hurricane Iniki."

"I've tried sleeping with earplugs, but it doesn't work. I can still hear him."

"Ho, brah, maybe you try somethin' else take your mind off." Spider legs kicked when he winked. "A nice wahini, maybe."

"That's what Lili said."

"She did? Huh. She mention her daughter?"

"Not in that way."

Larry D shrugged. "Makani is nani. Dat what we always say. Means beautiful. Her heart as big as Hawai'i." He paused. "Lili tell you what she doin'?"

"Something about working on a coffee farm down in Holualoa."

"She say when she comin' back to 'Ōlauniu? We miss dat girl."

Leo shook his head. "Odds are I won't be here anyway. My boss needs me in New Mexico."

Larry D scrunched his face again. "You know you got to pay for da whole month. You move out early, you still got to pay, brah. Dat was da deal."

"Don't worry, the company's good for it. Anything special about the special tonight?"

"Fo' shuah. My cousin got a boat. He got fresh opakapaka. Dat's pink snapper. Very ono. We also got 'opihi."

"What's opihi?"

"'Opihi, like Hawai'i, not Hawaii. We make a bruddah out of you yet." He grinned. "It a little shellfish dat clings to rocks in hard to get places. Anothah cousin get up early and go down to Ka Lae and pick them. Very dangerous because of da surf. Lotta people get killed doing dat, but it's worth it. Why we call 'opihi deadly delicacy."

"What the heck, I'll try them both."

"K'den. Ho, here come Lili. You know she hula here? She and three othah aunties. They da original queens. You watch, they talk story using only hands and eyes. Ask her when Makani's comin' home."

*

A couple of days later when Leo was leaving for work, Lili called from across the field. "Aloha, can I get a ride?"

Town was only a few blocks away, but it was on the way to the tower, which was five miles down the road. "Sure, no problem," he said.

She climbed into the cab. "You like this pickup?"

"It's okay."

"The color is wrong. Mo' bettah you get a red one, eh? It won't show dust so much, especially when you drive on red dirt roads."

"It's a rental. They only had white when I picked it up."

"You should take it back and trade."

"I'd have to drive all the way down to the airport and I don't have time for that."

"Kona not so far. Red mo' bettah, eh?"

"Maybe, but I'm not going to be here much longer anyway."

"How come?"

"I'm nearly finished with the job."

"How much longer?"

"Any day now." He slowed as they reached the Jade Empress with the cluster of storefronts on either side. "Where can I drop you?"

"Waipi'o."

"I don't know that store."

"It not a store, it a town. My cousin called. She sick so I go cook something special for her."

"A town? Where?"

"Not far. Take about hour half. We go mauka to Waimea and then makai to Honokaa and then down to Waipi'o. Very beautiful. You love it."

"But my job. I'll be late."

"The wind wait for you."

It was too late to say no, so Leo gritted his teeth and drove. If he pushed it, he could be back at the tower by the time his boss woke up in San Francisco. He was calling every day for a progress report. The two-lane forked ahead and Lili directed him to take the High Road. It was skinny and sinuous and coiled around the western flank of the island's oldest volcano. Soon they were snaking through clouds and pine forests and then across grassy fields dotted with grazing cows.

"What you think of the hula?" Lili asked.

"It was quite a show."

"The aunties and me danced together long time now. We used to go all over the islands and even won prizes, but now we dance only in 'Ōlauniu. The Jade Empress on special Friday night and weddings and funerals."

Leo concentrated on the road. There was little shoulder and big gaps in the guardrail. The drop-off was thousands of feet.

"How come you not married?" Lili asked.

"I move around a lot for work."

"Wherever the wind blows you, eh?" She laughed. "You meet the right person, it don't matter where you go. You always take love with you. The last hula the aunties and me danced, that what it all about. Our loved ones paddling away on long voyage and we sending our love so they always have it no matter how far they go, how long they gone."

When Leo didn't respond, Lili said, "My daughter Makani not married either, but she know all about love."

Leo couldn't think of anything to say to that.

They drove in silence as they crossed to the leeward side of the island. After Honokaa, the road dropped steeply. Leo put the transmission into low and pumped the brakes the whole way down. When they reached sea level, the smell of burning rubber and brake pads wafted into the cab. He rolled down his window so the ocean breeze would blow the stink out.

"Not much farther," Lili said. "We cross stream and then go up dirt road. See, why you need red truck. My cousin live near waterfall. You want to come in and have a plate when we get there? I make poke and pineapple rice. You could swim, you want. Waterfall has big pool at bottom."

"I got to get back to work."

"That's right. You always trying to catch the wind."

"It's my job. How will you get back to Olauniu?"

"'Ōlauniu," she corrected. "I stay until my cousin feel better and then Makani bring me. She has nice red car. Did I tell you she dances too? The aunties and me taught her."

"I don't think you did."

"Oh yes, she very good. I'm going introduce you when we get home."

"Well, I may not be there. Like I said, I'm nearly finished."

"But it depend on the wind, eh? Mahalo for the ride, Leo."

*

Of the different winds that blew on the Big Island's northern tip, the most uncommon was no wind at all. Locals called the condition mālie and everyone was saying it when Leo arrived back from Waipi'o. The trades had stopped that morning and the clouds disappeared. The absence of even a puff put the brakes on Leo's work. Though he was pretty sure he had fixed all the bugs, he still needed to run a series of final tests before the system would get the all-clear.

He waited out the day and then another. Still no wind. He reported the situation to the home office. His boss accused him of stalling: "The client picked that location because it blows there 24/7/365. What the hell are you doing, becoming a beach bum? Just give the turbine a pass and move your ass. I'll pick you up at the Albuquerque airport myself."

Leo had never cut corners and was reluctant to start. He decided to wait it out a little while longer. He stopped off at the Jade Empress. Steve, the bartender, had never come back from Honolulu, and so Larry D was still doing double duty. Since the old hotel lacked air conditioning, he'd bought a fan at Hasegawa Mercantile and set it on the bar with a bucket of ice placed in front. Then he strategically placed himself on a stool on the other side of the bucket.

"You want a beer, brah, help yourself," Larry D said. "It too hot to move."

"When is the wind going to start blowing again? Soon, right?"

"I don' remember a mālie last this long and I never lived nowhere else."

"But it will end."

"True dat, but who knows? Maybe all this because of global warmin' like all da hurricanes. I heard some haole on TV call it global weirdness. Mauna Kea got mo' snow than evah. You been up there yet? You can see forevah."

"I need the wind to start up so I can finish my job."

"Ho, brah, if I didn't have to work, I'd be chillin' on da beach 'neath a hau tree or paddlin' my outrigger to make my own breeze. You shoulda stayed in Waipi'o. It cooler there."

"How did you know I was there?"

"My cousin called and said you gave Lili a lift."

"Your cousin is the one who's sick?"

Larry D nodded and moved his face closer to the fan. It sent his wispy goatee and eyebrows skittering.

"Does that mean Lili's your cousin too?"

"We all cousins. You grow up here, you eithah a bruddah, a sistah, a cousin, an uncle or an auntie. It ohana. I'm uncle to Makani. She call me dat out of respect, not that I'm old."

"I'll take your word for it."

"You should go to da beach."

"If I did, which one?"

Larry D turned, his mouth open. "You not been to da beach since you been here? Ho, brah, dat plenny lolo."

Leo shrugged. "Work."

"You can' live in Hawai'i and not go to da beach. It, like, unreligious. Unhealthy too. Tell you what. Go to End a da Road Beach. It da best. You see."

The name made it easy to find. A few other cars and trucks were parked there already. A trail led down to a stretch of black sand edged by blue water. Several outriggers were pulled up on the sand. A couple of others were on the water, their paddlers aiming for the outside reef. No wind meant no sails. Leo went swimming. The water was clear and warm. He watched green sea turtles nibbling on seagrass, parrot fish chomping on coral. When he got out, he went for a walk along the shoreline. A trail at the end led up to an outcropping of lava. A grouping of rocks appeared to have been arranged by hand. A wooden sign spelled out "Kapu" in carved letters. He looked back at the water. The sun sparkled on it as if the surface was sprinkled with diamonds. He walked back down the beach and found some shade in a thicket of ironwood trees. He spread out his towel and dozed off.

When he awoke, the sun was setting and the sea turned red and then purple. On the drive home, he bought some bananas from a couple who was selling them out of the back of their truck. He mixed them with rum and ice and drank daiquiri after daiquiri while sitting on his lanai and studying the constellations. No matter where in the world he went, he always looked for them. He picked out his sister's namesake and then found his own. It was still hot when he went to bed, and so he left the door and windows wide open.

As Leo waited for King Kamehameha to trigger the garden light and crow, his thoughts began to drift. He checked off the list of all the places he'd been. Some of the job sites were near big cities, others way out in the bush. He tried to pick his favorites, but he'd never stayed long enough for any to become unforgettable. He never bought souvenirs, never took pictures. He couldn't picture the faces of any of the locals he'd met nor could he accurately place the few foreign words he did remember.

His thoughts eventually led to Berkeley where he'd spent his final two semesters taking a mix of engineering and environmental studies classes. He rented a room at The Stonehouse Co-op, a shared living residence next to campus. The co-op had been founded in the 1960s and still kept that vibe. There were 30 bedrooms, but all the bathrooms, kitchen, dining hall, and living room were communal. Clothing was optional and the hot tub a favorite gathering place for impromptu parties. When Pine and Luna visited him there, they wept for joy. "It's the Blue Bird on steroids," his father pronounced.

Leo was moving in his few belongings before the start of classes when a woman with bangs and a pierced nose appeared in the doorway. "You're new. You didn't live here last year," she said. It sounded more like an accusation than a statement.

"No, I was doing a semester in Spain, and before that, I was at UCSB."

"I hate Santa Barbara. All those oil rigs and tar on the beach. I have the room next door. I'm Sondra. Do you have a girlfriend?" When he shook his head, she asked if he was gay. Again he shook his head. "Word of advice? Lots of people in Stonehouse sleep with each other and it's always best to ask first and not assume. You don't want to be labeled a sexist pig."

"I'll keep that in mind," he said.

The next morning, he was taking a shower when the plastic curtain parted and Sondra stepped into the stall carrying a bottle of herbal shampoo. "We're all about conserving water here," she said. "Oh, you're not circumcised. I always find they look more eager that way when getting hard."

By the end of the first semester, Leo grew used to Sondra filming everything—film studies was her major. She accompanied him on a trip to Mendocino for Thanksgiving. His parents had parked the Blue Bird in a friend's driveway. Aries was there too, and she, Sondra, and Luna hit it off cooking tofu turkey and baking pot cookies. Pine told Sondra that she'd surely lived past lives and possessed the aura of Rati, the Hindu goddess of love. Leo went to meet Sondra's parents over winter break. They lived in a big house in Pacific Palisades. Her father was some famous movie studio executive. He asked Leo if his parents named him for Leonardo DiCaprio. When Leo said no, he said, "Tolstoy? Da Vinci? How about Leo G. Carroll? You know, *Topper*, *The Man From U.N.C.L.E.*?" Sondra lost it. "What's with the inquisition, Daddy? Leave him alone." Her father shrugged. "Just trying to see what kind of boy you brought home this time."

By the end of the school year, Sondra and Leo were talking about life after graduation, maybe even living together. The Film & Media Department held a screening of the seniors' final projects. Leo and Sondra sat at the front of the theater. Her film was introduced by an assistant professor who had a toreador's pigtail and wore a T-shirt with a picture of Luis Buñuel on it. He said Sondra's film was a bold, creative expression by an artist with the courage to pierce the veil of preconceived notions. The opening shot was of a camera on a tripod set in front of a keyhole. The next shot showed the room through the keyhole. The lens soft focused on a bed. As the focus grew sharper, it became clear two people were making love. Leo soon recognized his feet, his legs, and Sondra's back as she straddled him. The camera kept switching viewpoints showing the couple in different positions at different times—morning, nighttime. It never revealed their faces. And then the figures changed and it was no longer him, but a woman making love with Sondra. He could see a tattoo of a mermaid and realized it was the marine biology major who lived on the second floor. And then another scene change and it was Sondra with another man. Leo recognized the history major from Edinburgh's long red hair. And then it was the Indian guy who was always playing chess in the living room. And then the woman who dominated the Stonehouse's kitchen with her vegan baking. By the end of the film, Leo had identified a dozen of his fellow housemates.

A week later, he was bound for Saskatchewan on his maiden assignment for the wind power company.

*

The first thing he noticed in the morning was the rattle of palm fronds and the flutter of curtains blowing inward. Not only had he slept all night, but the wind was back. The second thing he noticed was someone calling "Aloha."

A young woman stood on his lanai. She held out a small burlap sack. "You must be Leo. I'm Makani. I brought you some beans from Holualoa. You got coffee filters? I'll put on water and make some fresh."

Before he had a chance to respond or rub the sleep from his eyes, Makani sidestepped him and entered the sugar shack. She showed neither embarrassment nor judgment at the sight of his unmade bed and the empty bottle of rum next to it. She found the kettle, filled it from the tap, and turned on the hot plate.

"You don't have a grinder, do you? No worries, I can make do."

She plucked the rum bottle from the floor, poured a handful of dark coffee beans on the kitchen counter, and began rolling.

"Necessity is the mother of invention, right?" she said.

"I'm just renting the place, so I'm not set up for guests," Leo said. "I'm not sure if there's even a second cup."

Makani turned around and flipped her hair over her shoulder. "Oh, I can't drink coffee now." She placed her hand on her stomach. Her smile was like her mother's, the foam of the breaking waves even whiter. It was only then that Leo realized she was pregnant. And very pregnant, from the look of it.

"Sorry," he said. "Of course." He paused and then hooked a thumb toward the bathroom at the rear of the shack. "Excuse me, I…"

"Take your time. I'll make the coffee and we can sit on the lanai and visit. Okay?"

He went into the bathroom and splashed water on his face and dragged a brush across his hair. The face in the mirror had bags under the eyes and a three-day stubble.

"She must think I'm a drunk," he muttered to it. And then he thought about her condition. "So that's why Lili's been so insistent I meet her. She said she wasn't married."

Makani was sitting at the little table on the lanai when he came outside. In addition to a cup of black coffee, there was a plate of sliced fruit in front of the empty chair. She had found the last banana from the bunch he'd turned into daiquiris and added papaya and mango.

"Thanks, but you didn't need to go to any trouble."

"What else am I to do waiting for it to be coffee? A watched pot never boils, right?"

"I'm sorry, but I got to get going. Your mom's rooster must not have crowed last night because I slept in and now I'm late for work. The wind is finally back, and I got to finish my job. They're waiting for me in New Mexico."

She smiled. "Try the coffee. Tell me what you think."

The aroma had already reached his nose. He could taste chocolate, wood smoke, and orange peel. He drank some. It was not burnt nor bitter nor oily. It was mellow without being sweet.

"It's very good," he said.

"Do you mind sitting down?" She gestured at the chair. "I'll get a stiff neck looking up at you. You're so tall."

Leo didn't want to get trapped into some kind of long, drawn-out conversation. He tried to think of something to say without sounding rude. "Just for a bit and then I really got to go. My boss."

"Good bosses are never bossy."

"I'll remind him of that when he calls to chew my ass."

She laughed. It was a good laugh. Real, unforced, and not too loud. He sat down. "Your mom told me you work on a coffee plantation. I take it you have a good boss."

"The plantation belongs to my best friend Noella and her husband James. It's on one of the steepest parts of Hualālai. When the coffee plants bloom and you look down from their lanai, the terraces look like they're covered in snow. It's so pretty. You should see it."

"Maybe if I ever come back to Hawaii."

"Try the fruit. I squeezed some lime on it so the banana won't brown."

He speared a piece with a fork. There was another flavor there, but he couldn't place it. "What do you do there? Pick beans, roast them?"

"I help out a little bit, but they have workers who are very skilled doing that sort of thing."

"I thought Lili said you worked there."

"Well, some might call what I do work." She laughed. "But I don't think of that way. I'm there to spend time with Noella and James so they can talk to the baby and when she's born, she'll recognize their voices."

"Oh, part of the auntie uncle thing, huh?"

"What do you mean?"

"Larry D told me how everyone on the island is a cousin or whatnot. So Noella will be your baby's auntie. I get it."

Teeth showed and the surf crested high. "I'm sorry, but, no, you don't." She placed both hands on her stomach. "I'll be the auntie. This is Noella's and James's baby."

Leo's mind churned as he tried to grasp what she was saying. When he thought he finally understood, he said, "Oh. Okay." He wanted to ask her how it had worked. Was it James's sperm or Noella's eggs or both or what. But he had the presence of mind to swallow the words and wash them down with coffee.

He felt Makani looking at him as if reading his thoughts and so, embarrassed, he dipped his head studied the plate of fruit. "I really got to get going. I'm late for work."

"My mom says you say that a lot. Leo's always in a hurry, she says. You know that's very un-Hawaiian."

"Well, I'm not Hawaiian and, besides, I got this deadline, see, and I got to make it. The company's counting on me. And not just them. Everyone who lives here too. Once the turbine's up and running, their power will be cleaner and their bills cheaper."

"By you catching the wind."

"Well, making sure the turbine does."

"You sound like you know a lot about the wind."

"I've been on the job for a few years now, so, yeah, I know enough about how it works. How to position a turbine and angle the blades for the most efficiency. How to control generation and feed the power into the grid. That sort of thing. Look, I really got to go."

"What about everything else the wind does?"

"What do you mean, *else?*"

She raised her hands and swept them. "How it gives life. Hawai'i and the other islands are volcanoes that sprouted in the sea. They're further away from a continent than any other islands on Earth. How do you think the plants got here? The birds? And people, the ancient ones? All the same way. They traveled on the wind. Wings, sails, currents."

"You sound like a teacher."

Makani smiled. "You caught me. I teach preschool. Well, I did until I took time off to become an auntie. I suppose, I've always felt close to the wind because of my name."

"Makani meaning wind."

"You speak Hawaiian?" She smiled.

"Not according to your mother or Larry D. They're always correcting my pronunciation."

"Did she tell you why she named me that?"

Leo shook his head.

"Because of my father. He had a job on a cargo ship. There was a big storm and the ship was lost at sea. Every day she would go to where your wind tower is, and when I was born a few months later, she started taking me too. We... " She seemed reluctant to finish the story. Or maybe her emotions prevented her.

Leo's mind raced trying to guess what it was. And then it hit him. "Not to look for your father, but to send a message to him on the wind. The last hula. She told me about its meaning."

"I guess I have no secrets now. Okay, it's your turn. Tell me how you got your name. Tell me something about yourself that I'd never guess."

That caught Leo by surprise, and he felt himself unable to resist. He told her about growing up on the Blue Bird. How Pine and Luna in trying to be so unconventional had foisted even stricter rules on Aries and him. He even told her about Sondra and the film.

At one point when they were talking, Makani grimaced and then smiled. "Oh. Oh. She's kicking. Have you ever felt a baby kick?" And when Leo admitted he never had, that he had always been far away during both of his sister's pregnancies, Makani beckoned to him and placed his palms on her stomach. "There. You feel her? She's saying aloha."

It wasn't until a feathered flash of red and gold and green caught Leo's eye that he realized the morning had passed and he'd forgotten all about the tower. The big rooster strutted right up to the lanai and cocked his head at them.

"Hello, handsome. Have you missed me?" Makani said.

King Kamehameha stuck out his golden breast and crowed.

*

Leo awoke at dawn on Friday morning. He made a cup of coffee from the beans Makani had left, and then drove to the tower to conduct the final tests. He ran a series of checks on the main power cable that ran down the inside of the tower. Then he checked the network of fiber optic cables that relayed real-time data from sensors measuring pressure, rotational speed, power, voltage, temperature, and oil level. He also tested the tower's exterior warning lights by simulating a series of disasters, including a tropical storm, an island-wide blackout, and a bird strike. When he was confident all the systems were working as designed, he contacted the home office and alerted the State Energy Office and Hawaii Electric. He ran the tests again with the officials monitoring them on their computers. Everything passed.

"All systems go," his boss cheered over the phone. "And now you go too, Leo. Text me your flight info. I'll see you in Albuquerque."

Leo stopped off at the Jade Empress on the way back to the sugar shack. Larry D greeted him with a "Howzit, brah."

"Tired, but in a good way. The wind turbine is good to go."

"Aw'right. Now we goin' have cheap power. First thin' I'm goin' do is buy AC for da bar. No way I'm goin' try and cool it down with ice cubes again." He pushed across a beer. "On da house."

"Mahalo," Leo said.

"Ho, listen to you. All bein' a bruddah now. So, when your

company goin' throw a luau."

"Luau?"

"Fo' shuah, we gotta have a luau. 'Ōlauniu been waitin' a long time on this day."

"The company doesn't do that sort of thing."

"What sort of thing?" a voice behind him said. Leo glanced over his shoulder. It was Lili.

Larry D answered before Leo could get a word out. "He say da wind power machine all up and runnin' and I say we gotta celebrate, but he say his company won' pay for it."

"Why not?" Lili asked.

"I don't know, they just never have," Leo said. "Maybe the utility company will once the turbine goes online on Monday, and it's officially part of their grid. I'll call their PR guy and suggest it."

Larry D made the shaka sign. "It's cool, brah. 'Ōlauniu wait this long, we can wait some mo'. Right cuz?"

"Of course," Lili said. "And it give us mo' time for cooking, especially if we going make kālua pig."

"Ho, man. I can taste it already. You gotta stick around fo' dat, brah."

Leo thought about his half-packed suitcase back at the sugar shack and the reservation he'd made with the airline. He shrugged noncommittedly.

Lili motioned to Larry D. "Bring me a mai tai. And don't forget the umbrella."

Larry D laughed. "Since when do you drink mai tai?"

"Since Leo finished his job. No reason we got to wait for luau to celebrate with him, eh?"

"Now you talkin'. Jus' remember you dancin' tonight."

Lili hoisted herself up on a stool next to Leo. She was a good foot shorter than him. "Makani told me you two had very nice visit. She say maybe the reason you always in such a hurry to leave is because you in a hurry to find something."

"You have a very nice daughter. What she's doing for her best friend Noella? Well, you're right about her knowing all about love."

"She sweet just like me." Lili flashed her teeth. "She also very smart. She tell you she teaches kekie? I think why she never got married. She like you. Married to her job."

Leo sipped his beer and thought about what he was about to say. "I think it'd be hard to get pregnant, bear a child, and then give it up."

Lili frowned. "Maybe for some, but this baby is Noella's and James's baby. And Makani is not giving up anything because she'll be the baby's auntie forevah. Sometime being auntie mo' bettah than being mother because… " She paused and winked. "Because it don't come with all the baggage. You know what I'm talking about, don't you?"

Leo figured anything he had told Makani had gone straight to Lili's ears. He was glad when Larry D came back with Lili's mai tai, so he didn't have to answer.

Lili took a sip and twirled the umbrella. When Larry D went to make a drink for someone else, she said, "Makani told me you said you know all about the wind, but you didn't know wind made Hawai'i Hawai'i."

"You mean the plants and birds and Polynesians from the olden days."

"Not so olden. It's still doing it. Wind brought you here, didn't it?"

Leo couldn't argue with that.

Larry D came back. "You bettah finish dat cocktail. Music about to start."

Lili pushed the unfinished drink away and turned to Leo. "I go dance now and see you later. You should stay and watch. One of the aunties go down to Hilo to visit her grandson so Makani going take her place. You should also keep your ears open."

"For what?"

"Bells, not chickens. Only time in 'Ōlauniu all the bells ring at same time is when a new keiki born."

Leo ate dinner at the bar. He tried not to stare at Makani, but everybody else was staring too. Partly because of how pregnant she looked, but mostly because of well she danced, how her expressive eyes were synchronized to her lissome hand and hip movements as she told stories along with the other aunties.

Larry D leaned across the bar. "I told you, brah. Makani is nani, but, ho, she look like she goin' be an auntie any minute now. Dat going make me a gran' uncle, not that I'm old."

*

Leo stepped outside of the tin-roofed sugar shack to the sound of church bells. The simultaneous clanging was so loud that it even drowned out King Kamehameha's cock-a-doodle-dos. He carried his bag to the white pickup truck and put it in the back. Then he walked across the field to the hen house where the big rooster strutted.

"Aloha, King. Now you really got something to crow about." He tossed the royal bird a handful of popcorn kernels he'd bought at Hasegawa Mercantile.

Leo climbed into the pickup and drove down the rutted driveway and turned onto the two-lane blacktop. He passed by the Jade Empress without stopping. He had the windows rolled down and could feel the warm breeze blowing across the northern tip of the Big Island. "A Kaiāulu, fo' shuah," he said to the face in the rearview mirror.

When he reached his destination, he parked, grabbed his bag from the back, and began walking. The trail led him down to the black sand beach at the end of the road. He found the outrigger with the name "Da Kine" painted on the stern. It was just as Larry D had described it. Leo dragged the canoe down to the water, pushed off, and hopped in. He gave a few strokes with the paddle before raising the sail. It filled with the breeze and billowed like a cloud. As Leo steered toward the outer reef where he could get a view of the spinning big blades set atop the tall tower, he knew the wind would not only take him there, it would also bring him back.

THE THINGS YOU LEAVE BEHIND

Robin and Sérgio considered moving out of the city after their second baby. They even spent a few Sundays looking at open houses in the suburbs. Sérgio took one look at the backyard of a 3 br + bonus rm rancher on a tidy cul-de-sac and said, "I wouldn't know what to do with myself in the country."

"It's hardly the Amazon," Robin said. "And the schools here are top-rated."

"But where would I find a place to drink a *cafezinho* with my friends and watch *futebol* together?"

"I'm sure there's a Starbucks around here somewhere." Robin knew how it sounded as soon as she said it.

On the drive home, Sérgio kept pressing it, saying their jobs were in San Francisco, not to mention all their friends and her sister too. "We'd be spending our lives in the car."

The next day, Robin met with a local real estate agent, and two months later they bought a house in the same neighborhood as their tiny apartment. It was a skinny two-story Edwardian that needed lots of work, but the kids got their own bedrooms and it was still within walking distance to the park and close to the pediatrician; their daughter had asthma. Before long Robin stopped dreaming about modern kitchens with six-burner stoves and granite countertops.

The night Robin's sister was bringing her new boyfriend over for dinner Sérgio got home late. Robin said, "Where's the olive oil? Mona will be here any minute."

"What olive oil?" he said.

"I texted you to pick some up on your way. I need it for the *macarrão.*"

He pulled out his phone and showed her the screen. "See. No message. Why don't you call your sister and ask her to bring some?"

Robin shook her head. "This new guy? He could be the one. I want to make the evening special for her. I'll go. I know the brand I like. Here, finish feeding the kids and set them up with a movie. I won't be long."

She backed the car out of the garage and headed for Whole Foods. Halfway there she passed a corner market. Hanging in the window was a white plastic sign with changeable red and black letters that spelled out "Frsh Deli GoOds." Robin doubted any would be, but she parked and ran inside.

"Do you have any organic olive oil?" she called as she walked quickly to the cash register while glancing up and down the unfamiliar aisles.

That's when the gun went off. Twice.

The clerk slumped behind the counter and a man wheeled around and jabbed a pistol in Robin's face. A wisp of smoke snaked from the black hole and the heat from the tip of the barrel felt as hot as the ember on the cigar her grandfather would clench between his teeth when he used to pick her up by her wrists and twirl her around and around.

"You got a car?" the man said.

Robin couldn't say a word. She couldn't even nod. She still had the keys in her hand, so she held them out.

"Uh-uh," he said. "You drive. Nice and easy."

The man slouched in the passenger seat holding a brown paper sack in one hand and the gun in the other. He had a tattoo of the ace of spades on his right forearm. Robin focused on it rather than the gun as if something as familiar as a playing card that she'd seen hundreds of times during Go Fish and Crazy 8s games could make everything seem normal.

"Don't forget to use the blinker," he said. "Nice and easy."

She pulled away from the curb. Nobody in the cars waiting at the stoplight looked over. People standing at a Muni stop never glanced up from their phones. No one shouted, "Hey, she's being carjacked."

Robin didn't lose it until the man ordered her to take the onramp to the Bay Bridge. "Please let me go," she cried and shook so hard the steering wheel jittered in her grip. "I have a family. A little girl and a little boy."

"Keep driving. Nice and easy."

She told herself the police would appear in the rearview mirror any second. Someone must have heard the shots. Surely the store had a security camera. Someone would've written down the license plate number, maybe even snapped a picture of it. A Good Samaritan could be following them right now.

The bossa nova began playing from the cup holder. Sérgio's picture flashed on the screen of her phone. Her heart raced as she reached for it, but the man grabbed it and flung it out the window. Strains of Brasil 66 sailed over the hiss of tires.

She gasped at the thought of all her family photos being run over again and again. "You didn't have to do that," she said.

"Shut up and keep driving," he said.

They crossed onto the eastern span of the bridge that had been built after the earthquake. It was painted bright white and had lights like a cruise ship's. Palm trees rustled in the center divider and the lanes were open to the sky. It gleamed compared to the old span. Robin told herself the police had other ways of finding her besides tracking her phone. The car's Bluetooth, its radio, the alarm. It was only a matter of time before she was pinpointed. Then there would be police cars and a helicopter. They'd put up a roadblock and the man would see it was no use and give up. Robin would have quite a story to tell. It might take a while before she spoke to strangers again or let the kids out of her sight, and if she needed therapy, well, insurance would cover it. She'd studied the policies and insisted they buy the preferred plan even though the monthlies were a little bit more.

But no red lights flashed. No blue ones either. No helicopter spotlight shined down from the heavens as Robin exited the bridge and left her family behind to wonder where she went and why she didn't return.

*

Robin first met Sérgio in Golden Gate Park. She was a runner and on weekends her route took her around the polo field where pick-up soccer games were always underway. One time a player sprinted off the field and quickly overtook her. As he passed, he turned around and started running backward. He was short and sweaty and wore his hair long.

"I see you every Sunday," he told her. "You always wear red shoes. Like my jersey."

She ignored him.

"You run like a vicuña," he said.

She didn't break stride. "What's that?"

"It's a kind of, how do you call it, camel that lives in the Andes."

"A camel, huh? Thanks."

His smile grew wider. He'd never had braces. Robin couldn't believe he didn't trip, and he was wearing soccer cleats too.

"If you saw one, yes, you would know I am paying you a supreme compliment. The vicuña has long legs and a slender neck and hair as soft as clouds. It is free and wild and the most beautiful creature on Earth." He paused and leveled his brown eyes on hers. "Well, second most."

As pick-up lines went, it wasn't bad, and Robin had to give him points for originality. Then there was his ability to run backward. Well, that wasn't to be overlooked either. She agreed to meet him later for a drink. He proved as charming sitting at a bar as he did running backward. They were living together within a couple of months. Their firstborn was a daughter and they named her after Robin's mother. When a son soon followed, Sérgio's dad received the honor.

On Sundays, Robin took Allie and Pietro to the park to watch their father play soccer. Sérgio always wore the bright red uniform of his beloved São Paolo Futebol Clube. He had matching jerseys made up for the kids too.

"I will teach our children to speak Portuguese and play

futebol and cook *feijoada*," he said. "And you will teach them about Martin Luther King and the Grateful Dead. That way they will have the best of both of us, and when they grow up, you and I will live together forever."

*

The Delta Highway was a two-lane blacktop with no shoulders built atop a causeway that kept the Sacramento River from drowning farmland. A three-quarter moon dodged between clumps of clouds, its reflection a sporadic band of light that wavered on silent sloughs. Robin was having trouble holding the wheel steady. There was nothing to block the wind that blew through the Golden Gate and picked up velocity as it sped across the bay and open fields. She had to slow down every time they approached the narrow bridges that spanned channels tapering and bulging like varicose veins. It was the only way to safely navigate between the gauntlet of protective concrete abutments that anchored both ends.

"That's the way," the man told her as they crossed safely over another. "Nice and easy."

Traffic was sparse, but when an oncoming car or truck did approach, Robin had to avert her eyes to avoid being blinded by headlights. Every time she did, she caught a glimpse of the gun and brown paper sack. Other than giving directions the man never spoke. He didn't ask her name or what she did or where she lived. He didn't ask any questions at all.

"Please let me go," she said again. "You can keep the car. Just take it. I'll get out and walk. I won't tell anybody anything, I promise. Just let me go. Please? I have a child with asthma. My youngest has nightmares. They need me. Please let me go."

"Keep driving," he said.

"For my family's sake. Please?"

He raised the gun. "I said, keep it nice and easy."

Robin bit her lip. She bit it so hard her mouth filled with blood. It was warm and tasted metallic and reminded her of the liver her mother used to cook and make her eat when she was in high school and got her period. But it wasn't the blood that made her gag. It was the realization he was going to kill

76

her. Maybe not right away, but eventually he would. She was certain of it. He would rape her and shoot her and bury her in a ditch and she'd never be found.

She knew she had to get away. She could open the door and jump. She could slam on the brakes and he'd hit the dashboard. Then she would open the door and run. She had on her favorite running shoes. She'd run so fast he'd never be able to catch her. Run into the darkness so he'd never be able to see her.

But the gun. He had the gun. He'd shoot her no matter what she did. Robin was certain of it. He'd weigh her down with rocks and sink her in a slough. Or he'd drag her off into a field and dig a hole and cover her up. She'd disappear forever and Sérgio and the kids would spend the rest of their lives wondering what happened, wondering if she'd run away. They'd wonder if she no longer loved them. They'd wonder if she might come back someday.

She didn't want them to wonder. She was certain of that.

*

One Sunday, Sérgio had a split schedule, so Robin took the kids to Stow Lake between games while he stayed behind to rest. The path through Golden Gate Park took them past people flying kites, practicing tai chi, and walking dogs. The kids had wanted a puppy ever since they moved into the new house and now they started up again.

"That one's really cute," Allie said. "Pietro and I will take care of him. You and daddy won't have to do a thing."

"We'll see," Robin said. It was what she always said when she didn't want to say *no*. "We'll see."

She signed the rental agreement for a pedal boat and a pimply teenager helped the kids on with their bright orange life jackets. They chose a blue boat with white trim and set off. Robin and Allie pedaled while Pietro sat on the rear-facing seat behind them. The lake was peaceful as they circled Strawberry Hill. They passed by the red pagoda with its shiny green tile roof. A half dozen pond turtles sunned themselves on the naked limbs of a semi-submerged tree. Pietro made quacking noises at a line of yellow ducklings paddling behind their mother.

"Watch out for the trolls. They'll grab you by the ears," Allie called out as they approached the stone bridge that connected the little island.

Pietro covered his head. "I'm scared."

"Stop teasing your little brother," Robin said.

Allie hollered to make an echo as they passed under it. When they were back in sunlight, she turned around. "Mommy, Mommy. The trolls have Pietro."

"Stop teasing," Robin said.

"No, really, look."

Robin turned around. An empty orange life jacket bobbed in the shadow of the bridge. She ordered Allie to stay put and then scrambled over the back of the slick plastic seat and jumped.

The water was cold and slimy and dark. Robin reached the life jacket in a few strokes, but Pietro was nowhere to be seen. Another pedal boat was coming. "Help," she screamed. "My child fell overboard. He can't swim."

And then she dove, her eyes wide open, her arms outstretched. Her clothes tightened around her, and for the first time, her red running shoes felt heavy as stones. She ignored the burn in her eyes and the choking in her throat as she tried to peer through the gloom. Something bumped her. Instinctively she knew it was her child. She gathered him up, clasped him to her breast, and kicked to the surface.

Later, when they were home and the kids were asleep, Robin told Sérgio she had never been so scared in her life. "I thought I'd lost him. The whole thing didn't last a minute, but it seemed to go on forever."

"It was an accident," he said. "You saved our son and now it's over."

"But I left Allie alone in the boat."

"You had no choice. She was safe. She had her life jacket on."

"But it could've come off like Pietro's did."

"But it didn't."

"I was so scared." She shuddered and started to shake all over again.

Sérgio rubbed her back. "Yes, but never be frightened in front of the children. I don't want them to grow up to be afraid. I want them to always think of their *mamãe* as strong and fearless." He kissed her. "And fast and beautiful. Like a vicuña."

*

Robin's mind raced. She had driven this road before. She was sure of it. It was a couple of years ago. They had come out this way in spring. What for? To pick berries? A Sunday drive? And then she remembered. It had been a field trip for Allie and Pietro's school. She had volunteered to be one of the parent chaperones. She and Pietro sat in the front seat while Allie and two of her classmates rode in the back. They visited a farm. The farmer drove a green and yellow tractor and pulled them around on a flat trailer with big tires. They sat on hay bales and sang "Old MacDonald." They petted goats. Some of the kids tried milking a cow. Allie did. She wasn't afraid. The boys made crude jokes to cover their embarrassment touching the teats. Everyone fed dried corn to the chickens. They picked wax beans too.

Where was it? Had she passed it already or was it still up ahead? She recalled a narrow bridge anchored by an abutment and the turnoff onto a gravel road just on the other side that led to a white house and weather-beaten barn surrounded by green fields.

She remembered there was an enormous black bull grazing in the fenced pasture next to where the parents parked their cars. The beast terrified Pietro and the boy refused to get out no matter how hard Robin tried coaxing him. One of the other parent drivers, a father, came over and scolded Pietro for being a baby. He said the bull wouldn't chase him so long as he didn't wave anything red. And then the man laughed. The boy was wearing his São Paolo Futebol Clube jersey. Robin pushed the man away and told him to go. He reddened and muttered "bitch" before leaving. As soon as the man was gone, Pietro jumped out of the car and hugged her. Later, he petted the goats and even milked the cow.

The three-quarter moon slipped from behind a cloud and turned the two-lane blacktop into a river of milk. Inside the car, the dashboard lights revealed the clock. It was growing late. She'd been driving for hours. It was way past Allie and Pietro's bedtime. Sérgio must be frantic. Mona and her boyfriend too. She didn't want them to worry. She didn't want them to wonder.

The man glanced over. The light revealed the speedometer's steady climb. "Hey, slow down," he said. "I told you. Keep it nice and easy."

"We'll see," said Robin.

She focused on the approaching concrete abutment that protected the narrow bridge's entrance from wayward cars. In the moonlight, she could see a black bull. She could see a white farmhouse. She could see green fields beyond filled not with goats or chickens or dairy cows but a brave and beautiful vicuña running fleet and free. As she pressed her red running shoe down hard and aimed for the abutment, she knew Sérgio and the kids would always see a vicuña too.

DESPERADOS

The rental car bucks every time Gina speeds over a cattle guard, and she's hoping the shocks on the little Korean piece of shit were already shot when she picked it up and not that she's knocked the front end out of alignment. She tells herself she better slow down, that if those black beasts staring at her decide to stampede, it won't be trying to sneak a pair of pigeon-toed wheels past the Hertz check-in guy she'll have to worry about. She taps the brakes as she approaches the next steel grid embedded in the gravel road, but the bumpety-bump knocks her red-framed glasses down her nose. She's doesn't let go of the steering wheel to push them up, just tilts her head back and keeps her foot on the gas.

Gina hates being late, but it's not her fault this time because she had no control over the flight from San Francisco leaving two hours late or Google telling her the drive from the Reno airport would take half as long as it actually did. She hates that she's going to have to rush the interview in order to make her return flight. She hates that her producer was right when he told her it would be quicker to drive than fly. And most of all, she hates that she'll have to suffer his chinless I-told-you-so look when she gets back.

When she rounds a curve she slams on the brakes and the POS fishtails and the kicked up gravel hitting the wheel wells sounds like buckshot pinging off a road sign. "You've fucking got to be kidding me," she says out loud.

Gina pushes her glasses up to take in the view. A ranch house and barn perch on top of a hill overlooking lush green pastures. Jagged snow-capped peaks poking a cloudless sky as blue as she's ever seen form a screensaver backdrop. She rolls down the window and snaps a photo. She considers getting out and taking a selfie and posting it on Instagram, but decides she's already late enough as it is and better keep moving.

The scene grows even more storybook when she drives through a set of open iron gates beneath an entranceway made of roughhewn timbers. The drive leading to the house is lined with boulders that glint in the sun. She parks and takes in the fat bushes of wild roses that frame a shady front porch. A flurry of small brown birds is feeding on insects stuck to puffs of cobwebs that cling to the eaves like trapped smoke. It's the perfect metaphor, she realizes, just what she needs for the opening to set the mood for her latest legend buster: exposing a famous old west outlaw as a fake.

Gina notices she's getting no bars when she clicks her phone's voice memo to record a first impression. She hums the *Deliverance* theme song and laughs. Before she can climb the steps to the front door, some poor creature starts bawling from the other side of the barn. It leads her to a corral where a lean man wearing faded jeans and a straw cowboy hat with a gray feather stuck in the band is shooing a cow into a holding pen.

"Come on now, girl," he's saying gently. "There you go. There you go."

He loops a rope around the cow's neck and ties it off to the front of the pen. Then he circles back and ties another rope around a hind leg and throws the end over the top rail. He slaps her on the haunch and gives the end of the rope a sharp tug. The cow lurches forward and kicks. He yanks on the make-shift pulley to cock her leg, so the hoof stays off the ground. The cow's eyes roll back and green snot blows from her flaring nostrils.

My god, Gina says to herself, *a real live fucking cowboy right out of the wild, wild west*. She approaches and launches into her cover story, talking like she drives, introducing herself, saying she's the one who called and is working on a profile for an online magazine, not mentioning the name or that its mission is to rip the patina off historical figures like Confederate generals and slave-owning founding fathers, that she's grateful he's taking the time to meet with her, and what's that he's doing to that poor cow anyway, yanking her leg up like that?

The man doesn't say a word as he finishes tying a knot. The cow makes a few more pitiful bawls, but finally settles down when she finds a feed bag hanging from a railing. Trussed and standing on three legs doesn't keep her from burrowing right in. The man finally turns to face Gina. He's got eyes the color of his jeans and his face is tan and creased. She can't tell how old he is. He could be thirty, he could be fifty. She wonders if he has a full head of hair beneath that cowboy hat and makes a mental note to ask him what kind of bird feather that is stuck in the hatband and if it has any significance. The chinless wonder is always telling her that it's the little details that separate a great exposé from tabloid filler.

The man's wordless stare unnerves her and she's guessing he's pissed because she got there so late. Then she starts thinking maybe she's at the wrong place altogether, that maybe she should've taken a right off the two-lane instead of a left. It wasn't like the road had a name. There was an entire forum devoted to horror stories about GPS misdirects.

Gina sweeps her phone behind her back. "Is this the Wild Rose? I'm Gina. Are you Micah? We spoke earlier."

The man studies her a bit longer and then nods. "You might want to take her easy when you're off the blacktop. A car like yours doesn't have much clearance for ruts and rocks, much less four-wheel drive to pull yourself out if you go into a ditch."

Gina looks at her feet. She'd bought some cowgirl boots for the occasion, and now they look stupid. Of course he would've seen her coming. He'd have to be blind to miss the dust devil the crappy recycled beer can kicked up.

"My plane was late," she says. "I didn't want to keep you waiting."

"I wasn't." Micah's tone is flat, matter-of-fact. "Neither was she." He hooks a thumb at the cow.

Gina smiles, making a note that she could start the piece off with a clip from *Shane* or one of Eastwood's flicks. A tall, quiet stranger with a past; acts only when provoked; saves the town then rides off into the sunset, his own moral code keeping him from taking the preacher's wife with him no matter how much he wants to, how much she wants him to. And then a quick cut to the final scene in *Blazing Saddles* where Cleavon Little and Gene Wilder ride their horses into the sunset only to dismount and get into a chauffeur-driven Cadillac.

She'll find out if Micah's for real or not, just as she'll find out that his great-great-great-grandfather Ezra Rose was no Robin Hood in spurs, only a back shooting cattle thief who spent his loot on building this gorgeous ranch. *It's straight out of a fucking movie set*, she can hear herself telling the chinless wonder when she gets back to the office. *Picture it in Technicolor. No, make that Panavision like Tarantino used. It's widescreen all the way. I shot plenty of handheld, but what we really need to do is hire a drone for a flyover. It'll be killer.*

Gina pulls her phone back around and taps the recorder. "Can we get started with the interview? Let's make sure I have your name spelled correctly. Micah Rose. M-I-C-A-H. That's from the old testament, right? Wasn't he a prophet?"

"All I know is it's the name of a mineral that gives granite its sparkle. My parents weren't too good at spelling."

His face stays straight and she can't tell if he's making fun of her or not. "Okay, let me ask you this. Ezra Rose was your great-great-great grandfather. Three greats, right?"

"Can we hold up for a second? There's something I need to finish first." Micah pats the cow. "She stepped on a rock and her hoof needs fixing."

Gina holds the phone close to her lips and says "cow-whisperer."

"Is that bad?" she asks him.

"Can be. If it gets infected and spreads, she'll come down with fever. Once that happens, well, rain always runs downhill, doesn't it?"

"That's great," Gina says. "I mean, what you said about the

rain, not what's happening to the poor cow." She makes a frown.

Micah is staring at her, but his expression doesn't change. "Why don't you take a look around why I fix her up." He nods at a stand of aspens whose heart-shaped leaves are on their way to yellow. "That's as good a place to start as any."

She can make out a cluster of headstones poking from the ground like teeth. Then she checks her watch and calculates how long she has before she needs to head back to the airport. "Why's that?"

"You're after Ezra Rose's story like all the others. Truth lies there, not in some old dusty newspaper account or a kid's comic book."

"What others? From what site?"

"Let me see, one guy was writing his Ph.D. dissertation on the Sierra Valley, another was a librarian of some kind, and a couple of history magazine types. I don't remember the titles."

"What did you think of their pieces?"

"I didn't. I never read them."

Gina relaxes when she realizes no one's scooped her. Online content was so crowded now, everyone competing for clicks and ads, well, you never knew. She stares across the yard, registers how peaceful the aspen grove looks, the entire ranch for that matter. She tries to see herself living here, a technique she'd read about by a blogger whose hook was posting from every country in the world. Riding a two-hump camel in Mongolia. Making cigars in Cuba. Experiential writing, he called it. Or maybe it was existential. Whatever. Okay, it's not hard to see the ranch is definitely different compared to her apartment in a noisy building on a street that's even noisier. And working here? Different with a capital D. No phones, no screens, no Wi-Fi. How would she keep up with all the emails and texts, populate her blog, Facebook, and Twitter accounts? Stay silent a day and people will think you're dead. Worse, they'll forget you ever existed.

Gina checks her watch again. "How about if I help you with the hurt cow instead? I can ask you questions and it'll save us time."

"Time's for spending, not saving," Micah says.

"That's great," she says and checks to makes sure her phone captured it.

Micah disappears into the barn. Gina hesitates before following. By the time she decides to go in after him, he returns with a leather bindle. He lays it on the ground next to the metal pen, unfastens the ties, and unrolls it like a sleeping bag. It's lined with sheepskin and has loops that hold shiny silver tools. There are pliers with different shaped noses, wooden handled tongs, metal clippers, and a variety of saws and knives, some with straight blades, others with curved.

Gina puts her hand to her throat. "Are you going to cut off her leg?"

"Not unless the knife slips." He gives it a beat. "The rock punctured the soft tissue under her hoof. I have to open it up."

"Oh, good. I mean, not amputating it. Does this sort of thing happen often?"

"Goes with running three hundred head."

"That's all? It looks like thousands down there."

"It's all the pasturage can support. We're grass-fed Black Angus here. The operation's half yearling steers, half cow-calf pairs."

"We? I didn't know you were married and had kids." When he gives her a look, she adds, "Uh, that's what I was told anyway."

"It's a pretty big spread for one person to run, so I have some hired hands."

"What can I do to help fix her foot?"

"Hoof. Cows don't wear tennis shoes. You'll want to put your phone away because you'll need both hands if you're going to be of any help."

As much as Gina wants to record it, she does what he asks. Micah straddles the cow's cocked leg with his back pressed against her hindquarters and pins the fetlock between his knees.

"First thing, hand me those tongs. Second pair from the

right." He points them out, not bothering with pleases and thanks.

He clips the edges of the hoof. Next, he asks her for a knife with a short, curved blade and cleans and trims the sole. Then another blade.

"Here comes the tricky part. Grab hold of her pastern. That's the part of the leg right here between the hoof and fetlock." When Gina hesitates, he says, "I'm pretty sure she won't bite."

"Pretty sure?"

"Pretty," he says.

She laughs, makes a note to remember *dry and wry,* and wonders how she's going to be able to hold still a cow the size of her rental car, hoping it doesn't kick her or knock her to the ground. Gina's never been big on animals. She hates going to people's houses who have dogs that are always dropping a slobbery ball in her lap or humping her leg. Even worse are cats, especially owned by the other single women she knows. The only thing worse than writing a cliché is being one. She puts her hands around the cow's leg and holds on. She and Micah are so close together now their shoulders and foreheads touch and she starts thinking that maybe he planned this all along. She can hear her breath and wonders if he's hearing it too.

She laughs self-consciously. "This is hard work."

But he doesn't reply, acts like he's forgotten she's even there as he saws the blade around the cow's sole horn and then slips the point beneath the lip of the hoof and pries the sole open like it's the top of a tin can. The abscess beneath is purplish and domed like a mushroom. When he slits it, pus the texture of curdled milk oozes out.

"Ugh." Gina can't keep from turning her head.

Micah dabs the wound with gauze and then squirts ointment from a plastic squeeze bottle with a red nipple. He brushes plastic cement around the edge of the sole horn and pushes it back in place, holding it firm while it dries and sets.

"Okay, that's it. You can let go now."

Gina pushes up her red-framed glasses with the back of her wrist. Her hands smell like the park after they've spread fertilizer. "Is she going to be okay?"

"It all depends if the infection spreads. I'll keep her in a stall for a couple days. There's a faucet over there you can use to wash up."

The pump is the old-fashioned kind and Gina has to work the handle a few times before the water comes pouring out and splashes into a grinding rock set beneath. The water is icemaker cold and turns her skin pink as she rubs her palms together.

Micah brings her a towel. As Gina dries her hands, she looks at the long valley below. "Have you always lived here?"

"Mostly. I went to school at Davis, did a stint in the service."

"Military?"

"Army."

She makes a note to call it cavalry. "And your father and his father before him, they all lived here too?"

"That's right."

"All the way back to Ezra Rose who built this ranch," she says. "The outlaw."

Micah is gazing down at the valley too. Cows are wading hock-deep in grass. A pair of enormous gray birds are spiraling overhead. "When he needed to be, sure," he finally says. "But mostly it was others who needed him to be one."

Gina has interviewed politicians and celebrities, so she knows doublespeak when she hears it. She lets it go, thinking she won't start challenging him about Ezra Rose's supposed exploits until close to the end. She's learned the hard way that if you ask hard questions too early, they can often be the last. The trick to busting legends is to coax the real story out and get those who long believed it to admit they'd been hoodwinked. And if Micah decides to blow her off, well, there's plenty of written lore she can poke holes in, ridiculous accounts about Ezra Rose outrunning a sheriff's posse, holding up stagecoaches, rustling cows, shootouts and gunfights, giving all his loot away to support a town. And then there are the old drawings in gazettes and dime novels she can use. The one she loves the most shows Ezra placing a wild rose on the grave of a man he shot.

"Can we see the cemetery by the trees now?" she asks.

Micah says, "Sure, but I have to ask you not to take any pictures of it, okay? The last fellow up here did that and it ended up in some kind of video game. I had people driving up and walking around looking at their phones and complaining they couldn't play because they couldn't get a signal."

"Geocaching," Gina says. "Or maybe Pokémon Go."

"Fool's errand," he says.

She's still holding the towel so she can't record it, but files away a possible subhead: "High tech meets high noon."

The footpath to the grove of aspens leads through a riot of wildflowers. Some have lost their blooms, others still hold them. The buzz from black bumblebees creates a sound like a radio signal between stations. Gina keeps her arms tight to her sides as she walks.

"They won't bother you unless you bother them," Micah says.

"Let me guess, you're *pretty sure* they won't."

He's walking ahead, so she doesn't know if he's smiling, but she thinks he might be.

The headstones are not surrounded by a fence, nor are they fancy. There are no sculpted crosses, angels, or baby lambs. The lettering on each looks as if it was chiseled by hand. There are no swoops or swirls on the ascenders and descenders, just plain block letters spelling out names and dates.

Gina finds the one marked Ezra Rose. The dates are 1833 to 1888. The second oldest birthdate belongs to a Joshua Rose, born 1835 and died 1850. Another marker also bears the name Joshua Rose, but this one was born in 1873 and died the same year as Ezra. The headstone closest to Ezra's is carved with the name Meaghan Rose. She was born in 1848 and died the same year he did too.

"You said Ezra wasn't really an outlaw, so tell me how

everyone got it so wrong," she says.

Micah reaches down and plucks a handful of pale lavender lupins that freckle the top of Meaghan Rose's grave.

"You have to go back to Oblong, Illinois. That's where the Rose family was farming when word spread that folks were picking chunks of gold off the ground out west. They sent their two oldest boys to bring some back."

"The California Gold Rush." Gina looks at the headstones and does the math. "You're kidding, right? I mean, Ezra was only, what, sixteen, and his little brother Joshua fourteen."

"Times were different back then and boys grew into men fast. The family was poor and there were a lot of mouths to feed. The parents probably figured they didn't have a choice."

"Then how did they get to California? Walk halfway across the country, which means climbing over the Rocky Mountains and the Sierra Nevada too?" She loses the battle to keep from rolling her eyes.

He nods. "Their dad gave them a rifle for hunting game and their mother gave them a cameo brooch to remember her by."

"So how long did it take them to make the trek?"

"About eight months, but they almost didn't make it. Joshua slipped while crossing the Platte River and Ezra had to swim after him. A blizzard stranded them outside of Fort Laramie. A wrong turn on the Oregon Trail left them wandering through the Black Rock desert for days."

"But they did make it."

"I wouldn't be standing here if they hadn't. When they reached Nevada City, they traded their mother's brooch for two pans and a pick and shovel. They hiked up a narrow canyon and set up camp on a sandbar where a mountain stream makes a turn."

"And let me guess. They stuck in their pans and, presto, they were filled with gold."

Micah is braiding the stems of the flowers. He looks up from his handiwork and says, "Are you after what happened or a fairy tale?"

"The truth," she says. "All of it."

*

Ezra Rose was hardened after eight months on the trail. He looked and acted twice his age, and didn't waste words or squander trust. Coming across a bushwhacked wagon train robbed his innocence. Encountering grifters made him wary of conversation. The dangers of the journey were lost on Joshua, however. Even though he came close to dying more than once, the younger brother maintained his boyish looks and coltish spirit.

The pair called their camp on the bank of a no-name creek Little Oblong and for the next four months toiled without a break, busting rock, panning gravel, and chasing glitter. They lived on acorn mush and whatever Ezra could bring down with the Sharps .50 caliber their father had given them. Despite all their hard labor, all their calluses, they didn't find a single nugget.

In late fall, Ezra decided they'd better pack it in before winter hit and hike down to Sacramento, maybe even San Francisco. He figured they could find work there until spring and then look for another spot to prospect. The morning they were set to leave Ezra knelt by the creek to fill his canteen. Something shiny flashed. He dove in and scooped up a handful of gravel. Lying on his stomach like a spawned-out salmon, he opened his palm. A gold nugget half as big as his thumb gleamed among the pebbles.

"We done it, Ez. I always knew we would," Joshua hollered when Ezra showed it to him. "We're gonna be rich. I can't wait to see the look on Ma's face when we pull up in a wagon heaped with gold."

They spent the next two months panning for more. It was as if the rains of autumn had washed down the riches of the mountains. When snow was falling more than it didn't and the creek was more ice than water, they agreed to take their findings down to Nevada City and register their claim. They talked about store-bought meals, hot baths, and clothes that weren't patched with canvas and stiff with dirt.

The Rose brothers buried half their take near the camp before leaving—seven of the 14 sacks of gold dust and a bag of nuggets. When they reached the bustling town, they made straight for the assay office. It was easy enough to find. A long line of prospectors stretched out the front door.

After two hours of waiting, Joshua grew dizzy. "I'm starving," he said, trying to hold onto his easy smile.

Ezra didn't want to give up their place in line, but he could see his little brother was hurting. He looked up and down the street. It was filled with drifters, whores, and drunks. He sucked his teeth. "Okay, go get yourself something to eat at the general store we passed. You get it, then you come straight back. Don't talk to nobody. You hear?"

Joshua leaned in close. "How am I gonna pay for it?"

Ezra turned around so nobody could see. He handed over a sack of dust. "I don't know how much grub is going to cost. Just give them a little pinch at first. Don't let them see the whole sack. Understand?"

Joshua grinned. "You can count on me."

When an hour passed and his little brother hadn't returned, Ezra's stomach turned sour, but the front door of the assay office was right ahead. He told himself Joshua probably couldn't decide between the candy jars and cracker tins. Inside the assay office, two men holding shotguns and wearing Peacemakers on their hips stood on either end of a rough plank placed across two wooden barrels. The assayer stood behind it. He had gray muttonchops and wore a holstered gun strapped outside his black apron. Ezra passed across a small nugget. The assayer didn't say a word as he dropped it into a glass beaker filled with chemicals. He scratched a couple of numbers down in a ledger with a quill pen, then pulled the nugget out with a pair of tongs and placed it on a scale.

"It ain't the purest I've ever seen, but it's worth its weight. Going price is twenty dollars an ounce." He stroked his chin. "Where did you say you got it?"

"I didn't," said Ezra.

He shook out the rest of the nuggets except for the big one

he'd found first. The assayer's expression didn't change as he performed the tests again and weighed each one. Then he tallied the total and counted out a stack of coins. Ezra shoved them deep in his pockets.

"That it, or do you have any more?" the assayer asked.

Ezra still ignored the big nugget as he pulled the six remaining sacks of gold dust from his pack. The assayer's eyebrows rose. He untied a sack and poured it into a tin container. He placed the container on the scale, scratched down the weight in the ledger, and spooned a sample into his beaker. His eyebrows went from raised to pinched. He set the container of dust aside, put an empty container on the scale and poured in another sack of dust. Again, he spooned a sample into the beaker. His brow was as furrowed as a freshly tilled field.

"Well, son, the nuggets you found are gold all right, but this dust ain't. It's iron pyrite. Fool's gold. Sorry, but you're not the first to be mistook. Nuggets is easy to tell. Dust ain't. Don't worry. You'll learn."

Ezra didn't argue. He thought of Joshua and the seventh sack. He picked up his rifle where he'd been ordered to leave it at the door and bolted for the general store. It was jammed with people clamoring for supplies. Knowing his little brother had as much patience as sense, he ran back outside and started ducking into the clapboard buildings and canvas tents that lined the street.

"Joshua Rose," he called in to everyone. "Are you here?"

Finally, he reached a windowless shack with "Saloon" scrawled above the open door in crude black letters. Laughter and jeers were pouring from inside. Ezra took a look. Card sharks and a dozen miners crowded around a table. The room stank of beer, sweat, and vomit. Joshua was tied to a chair set atop the table. A thick man wearing a bowler hat with a stain on it that looked like he'd walked beneath a swallow's nest stood behind him. He thrust his hand under the boy's chin and yanked it upwards. Ezra's little brother's lips sparkled with gold dust, his eyes flashed with fear.

"They call it fool's gold, but it ain't fooled me," the man shouted with a whisky roar, his face the color of uncooked meat. "Only a lowdown lying thief would try to cheat a man in his own saloon. What do you say, gents? Should I give him another taste of his own medicine?"

The mob bellowed their approval.

The man forced open Joshua's mouth and started to empty the bag. The boy tried to twist and turn, but the ropes held him fast. His nostrils plugged and his mouth filled. He fought for air, but the more he struggled, the more he swallowed. His once bright eyes bulged.

Ezra shouted for the saloonkeeper to stop, but his pleas were drowned by hoots and hollers. He tried pushing through the mob, but no one budged. The man in the bowler hat kept pouring even though Joshua's feet stopped kicking, his body quit twitching. Ezra shouldered the Sharps and took aim. The echo from the .50 caliber rolled on like a thunderclap. The bowler hat with the stain on it somersaulted through the air as if blown by a cold wind and the men jumped back as its owner thudded at their boots.

Ezra used the rifle to batter his way to his little brother. No one dared stop him while he cut the ropes and carried Joshua out of the saloon, dust as golden as a sunbeam pouring from the dead boy's mouth. He found a blacksmith shop and bought two horses, tied his brother across one, and climbed aboard the other. Back at Little Oblong, Ezra dug up the second bag of nuggets and then rode up the canyon to the stream's headwaters and buried Joshua Rose on a hill studded with aspens that overlooked a grassy field spangled with wildflowers.

A sharpshooter with a sheriff's posse shot Ezra's horse out from under him the next day as he rode east to tell his parents their son was dead. As he lay dazed and bloodied on the rocky ground, the sheriff and his three deputies seemed more intent on robbery than justice. A fight broke out when they found the gold coins and bag of nuggets. In the melee, one of the deputies got knocked out. Ezra snatched his gun, fired it once in the air, and then leveled the barrel at the others who were locked in wrestler holds. When he ordered them to give back his gold, they went to draw their guns. Ezra shot them before they cleared their holsters. Two were dead and the sheriff was gut shot.

Realizing he could never return to his parent's farm, Ezra grabbed his gold, took the posse's horses, and galloped south. He wound up in El Paso and spent all but the big gold nugget on cattle. He drove the herd west on the Santa Fe Trail. When another drover tried to steal his cows, Ezra turned the tables on him and added the rustler's herd to his own. He sold the cattle in a sleepy Mexican pueblo that one day would become Los Angeles. Ezra took his profits and returned to El Paso to buy an even bigger herd.

The second night he was there, a man stepped out of the shadows as Ezra walked by and coldcocked him with the butt of a pistol. When he came to, he discovered his gold nugget was gone. He learned the thief had caught the morning stage, so he saddled his horse and raced after him. Ezra caught up to the stage and rode alongside to ask the driver to stop, but the shotgun rider mistook him for a bandit and let loose with both barrels. As Ezra slumped on his horse, the driver whipped his team to go faster. They didn't get far. A shoulder full of lead pellets didn't stop Ezra from using the Sharps to bring down the lead horse. When he reached the coach, he told the driver the real bandit was inside. He ordered the man to come out and hand over his gold nugget. The thief pulled a derringer instead and so Ezra shot him dead. He retrieved the nugget and gave the driver a hundred dollars to buy a new horse.

Ezra bought and drove cattle west two more times. The last herd he took all the way to the wildflower-strewn grassy field beneath the shady hill where his brother Joshua lay. He built a cabin right alongside and watched his cattle grow fat and multiply.

Greed not justice finally led men to him. A pair of prospectors working the no-name creek followed it all the way upstream. Ezra spotted them butchering one of his calves.

That night he appeared in their camp, the long-barreled Sharps in his hands.

"That creek will bring you nothing but fool's gold and misery," he told them. "Go back downstream if you like, but if you put one foot on my property again, it'll be the last step you ever take."

The men didn't doubt he'd make good on his threat, nor did they believe there was no gold to be had. They chased the glittering dust that danced in the water and filled bag after bag, hauling it down to the assay office in Nevada City only to learn the same thing Ezra had years before. More men dreaming of easy riches followed, each convinced they would succeed where others had failed.

Twenty years passed and a settlement grew up alongside the no-name creek. The people living there couldn't remember how the town got its name Little Oblong. They also forgot exactly how Ezra Rose had come to own the biggest spread around. Some said he'd pulled a chunk of gold as big as a boulder out of the creek, others swore he'd bought it with the loot he'd made from rustling cows and robbing stagecoaches. Ezra never bothered to set them straight. A reputation of being quick with a gun and unafraid of the law gave him the solitude he sought.

One day, he rode into Little Oblong to buy supplies. When he stopped by the general store a woman with hair the color of the wild roses that grew in thickets outside his ranch house was reaching for a jar of blackberry jam high on a shelf. It was impossible not to notice how her blouse as white as a Sierra snowfield tightened across her breasts as she stretched. Ezra went to help her, and in his haste, knocked the jar from her grasp. It broke at their feet. She crouched and touched the spilled jam with her fingertip and then put it to her lips.

"Sweet," she said. And then she touched the jam again and put it to his lips and laughed.

Her name was Meaghan O'Donnell, an immigrant from County Mayo in search of a schoolhouse where she could teach. They were married within the month. In a year, she bore twin boys. Little Joshua had the same smile as his namesake, the same way of making everything seem like a game. Cassius was more like his father. He had Ezra's rainwater eyes and wore his reticence like a suit of armor. Ezra clearly favored Joshua more, but Meaghan told him it was only because he'd never learned to love himself.

Family life caused some changes in Ezra. There wasn't anything he wouldn't do for Meaghan and the boys. He worked even harder and doubled the size of the Wild Rose. He built a new ranch house the likes never seen before. When his sons turned 13, he vowed to throw a party.

"We'll invite all the people from Little Oblong," he said. "I want everyone to know what fine young men my boys have become."

"But how will we pay for it?" Meaghan asked. "You just paid for the town's new schoolhouse. Lent money to the shopkeepers to rebuild after the fire on Main Street."

Ezra pulled the gold nugget from his pocket where he always kept it. "Now that I have you and the boys, I don't need this to remind me of what I lost that day. It's time I was rid of it."

News of the nugget and the party it bought traveled fast. Two hundred people showed up, some to help celebrate the birthday of the twins, others hoping to see what other riches Ezra might have. He butchered four steers for a barbecue. There were games, prizes, and presents. He salted a horse trough with gold painted pebbles for the children to pan. A band played and dancing lasted long into the night. The highlight of the evening was a fireworks show put on by a Chinese trader from San Francisco.

That night, after all the guests had gone and Joshua and Cassius were asleep in their room, Meaghan straddled Ezra, and with his sex inside her, pinned his arms to the mattress and stared deep into his eyes.

"Are you finally happy, truly and completely?"

"I am," he said. "I love my sons. I love you. I've never known such joy."

"And do you forgive yourself for what happened to your brother?"

"I suppose I do."

"Finally," she said, and began rocking back and forth, bringing sweat to her brow, her nipples cast in the light of the kerosene lantern next to the bed as gold as nuggets.

When Ezra awoke, he realized he'd slept later than ever. A smile crossed his lips when he remembered the reason why. He got up and went downstairs. Meaghan was in the kitchen.

"Where are the boys?" he said. "I want them to ride into town with me when I go meet the government cattle buyers. It's another part of the business they need to learn."

Meaghan laughed. "You'll only get Cassius. He's already at work in the corral. Joshua is still asleep."

Father and son rode off and were gone all day, returning home after sundown. The moment Ezra opened the front door, he knew something was wrong. He'd smelled the smell before: the acrid stink of gunpowder floating above the iron odor of spilled blood. One glance told him all he needed to know. Bandits, driven by stories that the big gold nugget was one of a horde, had tied Joshua to a chair and tortured him in front of his mother to get her to reveal where the treasure was hidden. When Meaghan couldn't tell them what did not exist, they killed them both.

The bandits weren't difficult to track. Not for someone with Ezra's years of experience finding cows that had wandered off. Not for someone with his coldblooded anger. He and Cassius rode all night and spotted the men at dawn. They were asleep around a smoldering campfire.

"Keep 'em covered," Ezra said, handing Cassius his old Sharps rifle. "If they make a move, think about what they did to your mother, think about what they did to your brother. There's no sheriff to help us now."

Ezra held a Colt .45 as he walked into their camp. He kicked the first one awake, and then the second, and then the third. "You can die right here or at the end of a rope in Little Oblong. It don't matter to me," he said.

One of the men had been sleeping with a gun in hand. He fired from beneath the blanket. The bullet caught Ezra in the chest, but he managed to shoot back as he fell. Laying on the ground, he heard a thunderclap like the one that had rolled through the saloon in Nevada City all those years before and then another. Listening to the echo of the Sharps roll on and on, Ezra hoped Cassius wouldn't blame himself for his death. He wanted to tell him how much he loved him, how he always knew he'd be the one to carry on the Wild Rose, but the voices of his wife and son and brother were calling, and so the words died on his lips.

*

The phone's vibration snaps Gina back to the moment. She glances at the display; the low battery warning flashes. She realizes she has a lump in her throat. Thank god the chinless wonder isn't here, she thinks, he'd be laughing in his hoody at her.

Gina swallows before saying, "What happened to him? Cassius."

Micah places the braid of lupins on Meaghan's grave and looks up. "I thought it was Ezra Rose's story you're after?"

"I am, but Cassius is part of it. So are you, for that matter."

"Well, Cassius never left the ranch. He worked it every day of his life. Grew it to its present size. He married late in life and had two sons. He's buried here too."

"Let me guess. He named his sons Joshua and Ezra."

"No. William and John."

"Is that because he believed the other names were cursed?"

Micah takes off his straw hat and runs his hand around the inside of the crown as if wiping away sweat. His hair is more red than blond. "I suppose that goes with being a writer, having an active imagination."

Gina bites her lip. "What about you?"

"What about me?"

"Are you a Joshua or an Ezra?"

"I thought we already settled that. Micah with an *h*."

"I mean which one do you take after? The lion or the

99

lamb?"

He puts his hat back on. "A lot of people say I take after my mother."

Gina feels the story slipping away. No way she can go back and tell the chinless wonder it was all a bust. For sure he wouldn't pay her expenses. He'd probably fire her too. There was always someone younger, cheaper, and more aggressive.

She shoves the phone toward Micah. "So, you believe the story to be true."

"Why wouldn't I? My father told it to me, and his father told it to him and so on."

"Then you admit Ezra Rose wasn't the big, bad outlaw he's made out to be. He's just a tragic victim of circumstances."

"Tragic circumstances, maybe, but victim?" He shakes his head.

Gina hears her father singing that stupid country western song he always sang when she was still dumb enough to ask his advice. Knowing when to hold 'em or fold 'em or walk away.

"In other words, he played the cards he was dealt." When Micah doesn't answer, she presses it. "Isn't that something you cowboys always say?"

"Maybe the ones in movies when the writers can't think of something better."

Gina shifts her weight. The damn boots she bought are too tight and she makes a note to change the line about him being dry and wry to rustic and caustic.

"You don't care how I portray Ezra, your entire family?"

Micah shrugs. "You're going to write or post or whatever you call it the way you see it. I can't change that."

"Sure you can. Tell me what you know, what you really think."

"I thought that's what I was doing."

"But all the stories about him, the legends, the articles, the mentions in history books. They make him out to be a Jesse James, a Billy the Kid."

"Like I said, people had their reasons."

She blows air out the sides of her mouth. "That was a long

time ago. Everything's changed. The last piece I posted got over a million views. It trended for nearly a week. The internet's everywhere."

"It's only where you want it to be."

"You can't not care about what others think. I don't believe it. You don't want to be trolled, do you?"

"You know, after Ezra died, those stories about him picked up speed some, but Cassius, he didn't pay them much mind. They didn't hurt nor help when it came to what was truly important. Making sure there was enough pasturage, the going price of beef, dealing with hoof-and-mouth, fixing the barn roof." He pauses. "I don't see it as being a whole lot different now."

"But what about protecting your family's legacy?"

"This ranch is their legacy, not what people write and say."

Gina's phone beeps letting her know he would soon be out of juice. "Okay, one last question. Who's going to take care of the Wild Rose when you're gone, buried next to everyone else?"

"To be written," he says, and the smile was all in his eyes.

*

Gina pushes the rental car to the limit, keeping one eye on the road to watch for wayward cows, the other on the rearview mirror. Sunset is turning the cloud of dust she's kicking up a smoky red, but she can still see the Wild Rose behind. She wonders if Micah's watching from the front porch and so she steps on the gas a little harder to show she's not afraid of running into a ditch.

She goes over the whole story, moving the different pieces around, trying to think of what she may have missed. Not much, she tells herself. Sure, she'll have to do a little digging on the internet when she gets home so she can fill some gaps, highlight some of the more outrageous claims. But other than forgetting to ask Micah about that damn grey feather in his hatband, she's pretty sure she didn't miss a single thing. If she has, well, she can either leave it out or make it up. Or maybe she'll call him and ask. He may not have Wi-Fi, but at least he's got a phone and she's not afraid to use hers.

WHEN MOUNTAINS MELT

The cabin was near enough so Will and Keri could go there often, but far enough so the city lights couldn't drown the night sky. They'd built it in a small clearing overlooking a creek fed by springs and fattened by snowmelt. It was simple, like their own expectations in life, just three small rooms heated by a stone fireplace. The rocks in it were mileposts of Will's career. There was a block of black basalt he'd lugged home from the Columbia River Plateau, wind-polished granite from the high Sierra, a wedge of sandstone once bathed by the Ganges, the fossil of a long-extinct fish he'd found in Montana.

They planned to stay longer than they normally did so Will could complete the update of a geology textbook he'd written years before. Keri hoped to replant a garden that had provided more joy than vegetables over the years even though it usually fell victim to rabbits and deer long before the first frost could claim it. But they put off such tasks on their first full day to take a morning walk instead. It set a pattern for the week. After breakfast they would throw sticks in the creek for the dogs, eat a picnic lunch in the meadow while blue jays scolded. They'd end the day with a glass of wine on the front porch to watch the stars and planets gather.

One morning as Will sat down to eat, his knees creaked louder than the wooden chair and he noticed Keri was wearing his reading glasses, which meant he'd put hers on by mistake again. The radio was on and a correspondent was reporting about war in a distant desert. As Will listened, he began to think about another arid part of the world. He could remember badlands streaked red and gold heaped beneath cerulean skies and clear water rushing through rocks spewed in Eocene times. He could hear the river's rapids and the memory of it soon drowned the babbling of the news. The fragrance of sagebrush replaced the coffee curling from his cup and the chair became a slab of shale salted with fossilized chips of mastodon bones set atop a painted hill where the vista of volcanic violence also held a vision of freedom, romance, and all the possibilities a young man could dream.

The original journey to that lava-strewn basin so many decades before had not begun as a scholarly quest to unearth the mysteries of epochal upheavals. Nor was it to decipher ancient pictographs left by a band of hunters who'd recorded the game they killed by painting cliff walls with fingertips dipped in blood. Will had gone in response to the kind of call that prompted migrating waterfowl to take wing and salmon to leave saltwater for fresh.

He first felt it as hints of a soggy winter's end began to show in furtive flashes of blue in wooly skies every time he spotted the alluring yet elusive river runner who lived across the street. First, there were neighborly waves from opposite front porches and then hellos when their paths crossed on campus. One night they sat next to each other at a communal dinner shared between two households of college students. As plates were passed, the river runner lamented the weather. She said she ached to shed her layers of fleece and rain gear and bask on a sunny riverbank. Will went in search of a map.

There were plenty of rivers he could've selected, but he zeroed in on one 200 miles east of campus. What drew him to Oregon's high desert was the high probability of cloudless skies, the surety of open space, and a good chance the river runner had yet to shoot its rapids. She allowed the river held intrigue after he unfolded a Forest Service topographic map, and when he said he could borrow a Jeep, she said she'd be packed and ready to leave at first light.

That night he dreamed of long days drifting through

languid pools and even longer nights camped beneath a canopy of galaxies. But when he picked her up, he discovered the truth about best-laid plans. Disappointment tugged at the corners of her azure eyes as she told him if she'd known his borrowed ride was a Cherokee, she wouldn't have offered to babysit a friend's entire litter. On cue, three Alaskan malamute puppies tumbled out the front door. Will realized that whitewater rafting with dogs too young to dog paddle was out of the question and paw pads not yet hardened to the trail scratched a trek on trails spiked with shards of schist. He swallowed his disappointment and told her not to worry, that they could car camp and teach the pups to swim instead. That earned a smile, but as he lowered the tailgate and installed the wolfish lookalikes in the cargo hold, he got another lesson. She took a look at the empty backseat and said it was a shame to let all that space go to waste.

An hour later they were finally on their way. The river runner was by his side, but two friends who seemed already packed the moment she'd called them rode behind. One was from Idaho and waited tables while waiting on her hometown's annual fiddle festival to strike back up. The other had emigrated from New Jersey. She pronounced dogs "dargs" and water "warder" and every time she laughed he heard a great blue heron call. Joni Mitchell soon elbowed Bob Dylan off the Jeep's stereo and the trio sang along to *A Case of You*. As they crossed McKenzie Pass, Will couldn't help but notice a solitary peak on the north while the snow-capped Three Sisters hugged the south.

His plan for finding sun appeared on track as they dropped down the eastern face of the Cascades and crossed a broad canyon. The Jeep's radiator hissed as they climbed the steep flanks of the Ochoco Mountains. He pulled into a vista point at the crest to cool the engine and walk the pups. Ponderosa pines soaked up the heat and their yellow bark gave off a smell of fresh-baked bread. A plein-air palette of color splashed below. The forks of the John Day River wrapped silvery reins around a caravan of humpback hills.

Will found a dirt road and delivered his passengers to a sandbar at water's edge. The women shed their clothes and left them shimmering like snakeskins on the beach as they dove into a deep eddy. Shivering and dressed in goosebumps, they scrambled out to warm themselves in the sun. The icy plunge didn't dampen the azure-eyed one's spirit any and she encouraged him to pitch a tent in a quiet spot at the edge of the campsite. He erected it in record time and then hurried back to the Jeep to fetch their sleeping bags. When he returned, he found her herding the pups into the tent, zipping it up tight, and telling them to stay out of trouble.

There was no other way to interpret the message, so he took a hike. A rocky trail led him upstream. Sunset was a few hours off and he began climbing as high as daylight would allow. Will covered the first mile fast. It wasn't until he slipped on a patch of scree and fell to his knees that he began to look around. Dwarf purple monkeyflower bloomed tenaciously among the glinting talus. Patterns took shape in the cleaved facets of the rocks. They told a scrimshawed tale of time and change. The ossified outline of a palm leaf pointed to tropical climes while the petrified branch of a mulberry proved jungle had given way to forest and then to desert. He picked up a calcified seed and then plucked an Indian paintbrush to examine them side-by-side. The distance between them was only two inches, but their origins spanned two epochs.

A canyon took Will away from the river. He climbed a steep sidewall striped with black, green, red, and buff bands. Each stratum was the rung of a geological ladder. In fifteen minutes, he traveled 50 million years. He touched sediments once drowned by seas, liquid basalt now hardened into the texture of asphalt, a river of volcanic ash and sludge that became a tomb for plants and animals that couldn't escape its path. The trail crossed a desolate scabland pockmarked by stony craters and whiskered with stubby sage. Will's goal was the top of a red hill that looked as if it had been swept from Mars by astral winds. When he reached it, he looked upon all that had been, all that was, and all that would be.

The sun arced high overhead as afternoon thermals sent cumulus clouds fluttering like sheets pinned to a clothesline. The land below had been forged by fire and sculpted by wind and water. It spoke of birth and life and death all at once. Will could see the once red-hot entrails of Earth, a crumbling buttress of a mighty stratovolcano that had surely turned day into night when it exploded, a river sawing relentlessly through miles of rock so it could ferry melted ice to the sea. Bird-filled willows crowded banks slipped by river otters.

The wildlife was a continuum. Once there had been rhinoceros-like brontotheres grazing here, this day there were deer, tomorrow who knew what kind of creatures would exist. The only thing for certain was everything that now appeared permanent was temporary. Gravity would pull, the continents would drift, mountains would come and go. The climate would change. Seas would rise and fall. Old would give way to new. That was the way of life. It always had been. It always would be.

Will put his ear to the ground and heard the echoes of the march of time trapped in the layers of restless rock. There was the trudge of amynodonts, claw clicks of saber-toothed tigers, footsteps of humans who'd crossed land bridges, rain dances around a campfire, drumbeats of hooves from cavalry troops, creaks of settlers' wagon wheels, and the hiss and hum of tires on pavement. They were all part of it, the ever-changing landscape, each and every one, from ancient animal to modern man, adding to it, taking from it. And in the process, the land had become part of who they were: ingrained, indelible, impossible to shake from body and soul.

He realized he was no different than all that had come and all that would follow. He was part of it too, the great journey onward, pushed and pulled by sun and moon, always on the move, sharing with plant, animal, and mineral a seat on a spinning ride through space and time. That something so big and grand as where he'd climbed could be so transformed in what amounted to the geological blink of an eye made him think about what lay in store for him. Not just that day or the next, but forever. As Will looked into the future, the only thing he knew with certainty was he would not be traveling alone. He was connected to it all: yesterday, today, and tomorrow, with the grains of dust on Earth to the stardust in deep space beyond. The rocks he touched were both grounding and freeing. As he vowed to learn more about them, he also vowed not to force into a weekend what a lifetime should take.

When Will returned to the riverside campsite, the bluegrass waitress was humming a melody that evoked more of Ireland than Idaho. The New Jersey transplant was sketching the canyon. The three pups had been freed from the tent and were watching the river runner tend a blackened pot warming on the embers of a cook fire. She greeted Will with a smile, her lips tinged umber by the setting sun, her azure eyes twinkling. She asked him what he'd seen.

Time, he told her. There was plenty of it.

Keri's voice pulled Will from his reverie. She said it was time for their morning walk and so they'd better get a move on. They gathered their things and headed out, the dogs running ahead to flush quail from thickets and send squirrels scampering up trees. When they reached the creek, the dogs jumped right in, their splashes and barks a counterpoint to the thrum and lap of water flowing over, around, and through rock. As Will listened he could hear a nasally twang singing a refrain about being so much older then and younger than that now, and he thought that, creaking knees and reading glasses aside, he felt the same way, especially when remembering the place where time was measured in layers of rock stacked old to new and where life had no bounds. He looked at Keri and, staring into her azure eyes, knew the river they were running still had a long way to go.

FISH RAP

Skip and me, we take the *Anna Marie* down to 'Frisco, riding the Humboldt the whole way until the current spits us out and we slip right under the Golden Gate Bridge as slick as you please. I say let's tie up at Fisherman's Wharf and see the sights, maybe ride a cable car, at least buy Betsy a souvenir, but Skip says the anchorage costs a day's pay plus we can't be late.

Copy that, so I keep the big Cat turning and smoke black as night belching out the stack as Skip steers us straight up the Delta. We're bucking a flood tide from two, count 'em, two rivers so chockfull of runoff the water's brown as mud. I say I bet if I throw a handful of sunflower seeds overboard we'd have big yellow flowers waiting when we sail back out, and Skip says, maybe toss some of that popcorn you forgot to sweep up from the galley last night and we'd have fresh ears to pick too.

We fall in behind a grain ship and ride its wake. Skip gets on the radio with some of the other skippers making sure they're still under way and didn't run aground or turn back when they saw how much fuel they was using, it being a 24-hour run down and no one's paying our bills but us. See, we're part of the North Coast fishing fleet, from Crescent City to Fort Bragg and every pothole in between, skippers and hands alike who can tell a troll line from a head rope and know where the schools make their turn for the Eel, the Mad, and the Klamath too.

We took turns standing watch last night, but Skip stood more than me 'cause I tend to fall asleep sometimes, 'specially when the Cat's purring and the deck's rocking gentle like. He's carrying more bags under his eyes than usual and I s'pose it's 'cause he's been awake so long and worrying about stuff some. Still, he took time to wash his face and comb his hair this morning like he does every morning, no matter if we're out a week or it's spitting nails and crashing whitecaps over the bow. Forty years running boats in the wind and rain, and he still packs Brylcreem in his duffle right alongside his gum boots and yellow slicks.

I ask how much longer and Skip says long enough. And when I ask what we're going do when we get there, he makes a sound like a whale blowing. Come on JoJo, he says, you didn't go and forget already, did you? And I duck and say just checking is all. He shakes his head and says we're going stick to the plan like that smart lawyer boy laid out. Tie up bow to stern in Old Sac and in the morning march straight to the capitol building and give the suits hell about how they might as well cut off our arms and legs if they go through with stopping the salmon season short again like they done the last three years running.

When I ask what'll we do if they don't listen and how am I s'posed to take care of Betsy and the little one on the way with no regular pay, Skip tells me there's no money in crying and he ain't about to let his daughter and a grandkid go hungry is he? So, I push my cap back and stick out my jaw and say, well, me neither then. Skip grows quiet for a bit and then says I better go down below and check the Cat's rocker arm. Sounds a little off, he says, clacking like. I swear he can hear a fish fart. Must be those hearing aids Betsy bought him even though he tells her there's nothing wrong with his ears that a whole lot less yapping about it wouldn't help.

We pull into Sac and the capitol building heaves into view on our starboard and it's gleaming white as teeth. I ask Skip if it's like the one they got in Washington DC and he says to quit my gawking and squawking and keep an eye out for traffic 'cause if we ram a yacht it's likely to have someone pretty damn important on it and then we'd be sunk for sure.

Old Sac is on the other side of another bridge, this one painted gold, even golder than the one in 'Frisco which is more the color of a crab trap buoy. It ain't as tall and draws up in the middle to let us pass underneath without knocking off our mast and antennas. When we reach the wharf we see a bunch of boats have beat us to it so we tie up at the end of the line but don't complain.

Some of the crews head over to a café for supper but Skip says we got to watch our pennies, so I heat the chili Betsy packed and Benny Hobo joins us. He's the skipper of the *Glory B.* out of Trinidad and I take an awful ribbing when I ask him if that's his wife's name like Anna Marie was Skip's before the cancer took her. Benny Hobo slaps his thigh and Skip makes the whale noise again before saying I got smacked good by a troll boom a while back so what d'ya expect. After dinner, Skip says I'd better get my 40 in since tomorrow is going come soon enough and I say that's a pretty good idea, so I say goodnight as Benny Hobo pulls a bottle from his coat and fills their mugs. I can hear them jawing as I kick off my boots and climb into my bunk. They talk about what skippers always talk about, the price of fuel is too high and the price per pound too low. They talk about the latest skipper to hang it up for good and when they start talking about insurance and how there's more than one widow and orphan out there who's able to keep the house thanks to a down with the ship policy, my eyelids grow heavy and I drift off.

Skip wakes me in the morning with a bellow. Where's the goddamn coffee, he says, and I say did he check the tin and he says of course he did, but it's goddamn empty. I can tell he's got a mood on like what usually happens when he and another skipper get together, so I tell him I must've forgotten to check it before we left. And he says how could you forget to do something as goddamn important as that, and I say it's probably because I took Betsy to the clinic the day before we shoved off and they took a sounding and we watched a screen like the kind on the fish finder and could see a baby in there all right. Skip makes the whale sound and says okay, okay, never mind, and how 'bout we go get us some real coffee and maybe a donut too before we give the suits an earful. And I say that'd be mighty fine by me.

We sit at a table by a window and I drink my coffee and look around. Skip and me, we're the only people in the place without wires dangling from our ears and talking with our thumbs. Everybody is dressed like they did their shopping at the same place too. Skip stares out the window at the early morning light and says when the sun's paler than piss, the rain can't miss. And I say what happened to ring around the moon, and he says a Pineapple Express is coming, and that's for goddamn sure. Going dump five inches easy, he says, and I ask him if he feels it in his bones and he says he heard it on the radio.

Seas'll be up plenty when we head back, Skip says, and starts nodding to himself like he does when thinking on a problem, whether it's what to do when the Cat quits or the trolling lines get tangled or a crab pot busts loose or how to talk Old Man Stansky into letting us fill our fuel tank and pay him later. I say maybe we should finish our joe and go say our piece so we can shove off early to beat the storm as I wouldn't mind getting back home sooner 'cause I'm sure missing Betsy already, but Skip smacks the table and sends his coffee sloshing overboard. Nobody's going tell me what to do, he says, not how fast to drink my coffee or how to fish or how to make a goddamn living. I keep my eyes on my paper cup as he talks. The girl who poured it wrote my name on it. She spelled it with two e's even though it don't got one, but she did make smiley faces in the o's, which makes me smile too. When I look up, Skip makes a face and says the cost of fuel costs as much a gallon as the bilge we're swilling and maybe coming down here was a goddamn mistake and he'll be goddamned if he's going beg a bunch of goddamn suits to let him keep his goddamn job.

I tell him we got to try, you know, because of Betsy and the baby coming. We got to talk them out of shutting us down, I say, and let them know guys like us are worth saving too. Skip shoots me one of his looks and then grabs a newspaper someone left behind and straightens the pages and starts to fold it. I been a fisherman all my life, he says, what do they want me to do, they take it away, open the scuppers and ride her down to the bottom so insurance has got to pay my family in full? He folds the top corners down to the middle, the top a triangle now.

Maybe they'll listen and it'll only be a week shutdown, I say, two weeks tops, just long enough to let enough fish get past. Skip keeps working the paper. Now he's folding the bottom flaps up on the port and starboard sides, the hook scars on his stubby fingers inching like worms. Better than telling 'em, we show 'em, he says. They wanna know how supper gets on the table, we take 'em out on the *Anna Marie*. See what it takes to find a fish in swells the size of haystacks. They'd puke on their shiny shoes, I say, but they'd never go. So maybe we do what that smart lawyer boy said, he says. We take a reporter and show the world how it's done on TV. He don't come, we record it ourselves. Mail the bastards a copy for all to see.

I slide my paper cup in circles and keep my eyes on the table. Download, I say, and Skip says what the hell am I talking about. It's how they do it now, I say. Download. To where, he says. And I say, to wherever they're going watch it, I s'pose. He blows and says, if you're so goddamn smart maybe you don't need to be a goddamn fisherman no more. Get a job pouring coffee like the crew in here. Have a steady paycheck and don't got to worry about drowning 'less you fall asleep face first in the pot. Be a lot better for Betsy and the baby, he says. And I say, no, I'm a fisherman through and through I am.

Skip finishes folding the newspaper and then makes the whale sigh again. Okay, he says, let's go give it our best shot then. We'll do what whatever it takes, he says, for Betsy and the baby. He stares at me hard. And I mean, whatever it takes, now or on the way back, he says, you with me? And I say, you're goddamn right I am. For Betsy and the baby. Whatever it takes.

Skip stands the folded newspaper on the table. As we're shoving off, a woman and man in matching suits climb aboard our chairs. She picks up the folded paper, her fingernails as red as her lipstick. What is it, she says, a paper hat? And the man shrugs and says, maybe it's a boat. I start to go back to tell them he's right, but then don't, seeing how they're laughing at how it's listing to port now, there not being enough pages in the want-ad section to make it strong and keep it afloat.

YELLOW DOG

Blowing rain sliced between the couple like scissors straying from a pattern. A passing car sideswiped a puddle and sprayed them with an oily roostertail purpled by runoff. Caroline didn't feel the splash. She was numb after telling Greta.

A flashing Don't Walk signal stopped them from crossing. Greta gripped Caroline's arm and leaned in close. "You sure picked a hell of a night to try and leave me."

"I told you, I'm not leaving, I'm going. There's a difference."

"No there's not."

Caroline didn't attempt to explain. Greta wouldn't have bothered to try to understand. It was one of the reasons she was going.

"Why are you ruining a perfectly nice dinner at my favorite restaurant?" Greta said. "Why can't you be happy?"

"You haven't been listening. I'm drowning."

"Are you trying to be ironic?" Greta laughed dismissively. "What's so wrong with what we have?"

"It's not any one thing."

Caroline looked at the sidewalk. Even their shadows cast by the streetlight were under water. She had loved Greta for three years and still did, but it wasn't enough to hold her any longer. When the Walk signal turned green, Greta held onto Caroline to keep her from stepping off the curb.

"Come on, babe. Don't be so dramatic. You're overreacting. Okay, I'll try harder. I promise. Let's go back inside and have another glass of wine. You can choose it."

Caroline pulled her arm free. "I'm not reacting. I'm acting for myself for once."

Greta's face turned the color of Don't Walk. "Then go. Go get your shit and clear it out of my house. But don't you dare touch my dog. And don't think you'll ever find anyone as good as me."

"Do you hear yourself? *Your* house? *Your* dog? See what I mean?"

A taxi was waiting for the light to change. Caroline ran to it and jumped in. When they got to the loft, the driver waited out front while she went inside. She threw clothes in a rollie and her passport in her purse. She picked up Frida, kissed her goodbye, and put her back on the couch. "Stay," she said. The Chihuahua started shaking and whining. "Oh, do whatever you want." And then Caroline closed the door and never looked back.

"Where to now?" the cabbie asked.

"SFO."

"What airline?"

"The international terminal."

The airport was crowded. Lines trailed from every check-in counter. Caroline looked at the screen listing departures and gates. London. Paris. Hong Kong. Bali. She pulled her wallet from her purse. All of the credit cards were joint accounts. Another one of Greta's ideas. They were plastic proof of her success as a partner in a big law firm and a constant reminder of Caroline's struggle to become a chef. She didn't want Greta to pay for anything ever again. All she had in her name was a debit card linked to a checking account she'd had since cooking school. She went to an ATM and checked the balance. She withdrew the maximum and added the crisp twenties to the ones and fives and tens in her wallet.

The agent asked for her ticket when Caroline got to the counter.

"I don't have one. Where can this get me?" She pushed across the wad of bills. "One way."

The agent's penciled eyebrows arched above seen-it-all

eyes. "It doesn't work that way. These are international flights. You're supposed to have a ticket already. I check you in, make sure you have a passport, and check your bags if you have any. Next in line, please?"

"Wait. Please, wait. I need to go somewhere. Anywhere. I don't care where."

The agent studied her. "What's wrong, honey? Man trouble?"

"Other way around."

The teased hairdo tilted. "You're giving him trouble?"

Caroline shook her head. "Woman trouble."

The agent leaned across the counter. "Honey, a dog's a dog. It doesn't need balls to be one. Let's see what I can do. Do you have any frequent flyer miles?"

Caroline gave her username and password and the agent entered it into the computer. "Well, there you go. You want to go tonight, right? How about Mexico? You have just enough for the flight to Zihuatanejo."

"Is it sunny there?"

"It's Mexico."

The agent's purple fingernails clicked when she tapped her keyboard. She printed out the ticket. "Here you are. And, guess what, it's your lucky day." Her penciled eyebrow didn't budge when she winked. "You got upgraded to Business."

Caroline rolled her suitcase to security and passed through without any hassles. She found two empty seats in the boarding area, laid her bag on one, and unzipped it. The clothes she'd stuffed in sprung out. She did a quick inventory and began sorting. Her favorite pair of jeans, shorts, some T-shirts and tanks, and a pair of sandals went in one pile. In another, the expensive blouses and skirts Greta had bought for her, including a designer sweater and heels she'd brought back as souvenirs while attending a law conference in Milan. Caroline folded those into a neat stack and placed it on the empty seat. She put everything else back in the rollie.

When she got on board, she pulled the shade down and fastened her seat belt. The plane sped down the runway and hurtled skyward. When it banked hard left, Caroline closed her eyes and gripped both armrests in fear she might spill out and tumble all the way down to San Francisco, through the roof of the loft, and right back into her life with Greta and Frida. It wasn't until the plane finally leveled out that Caroline opened her eyes. She'd finally done it. She'd gone.

*

The taxi driver had a Magnum P.I. moustache and drove a dented brown Nissan. He played *ranchera* music on the radio really loud. A family of *Día de los Muertos* skeletons rattled on the dashboard. His head was like an owl's, the way he turned and talked over his shoulder while he whipped around trucks belching clouds of diesel and accelerated past overcrowded buses.

"You hotel *es el mejor*. The best. Right on *la playa*. *Que linda*. Very beautiful."

"I hope so," Caroline said.

"And you wanna go somewhere tomorrow, just text me. *Restaurantes*, disco, shopping, anything. *Lo se todo*. I know everything." He took one hand off the wheel and handed her a business card. "I am Jorge. Ask anybody. *Jorge es el mejor*."

"I'll do that," she said, having no intention to do so. All she wanted was to check in, get into bed, and sleep. And when she awoke, roll over, and sleep some more.

The hotel receptionist wore a lot of product in his hair and smelled of cigarettes. "You are traveling alone?"

Caroline nodded and handed over her passport. "I made the reservation at the hotel's booth at the airport and paid for the first night in American dollars. Did you get the information?"

He shrugged. "It is in the computer, but people change their minds and bring someone with them."

"I didn't change mine." Caroline heard her voice, realized the words came out more curtly than she'd intended.

He handed her a plastic key card imprinted with a photo of bougainvillea. "You are on the third floor and have a view of the beach. If I can be of any assistance, just call on the room phone. If you need anything, anything at all."

Caroline turned around so she wouldn't have to acknowledge his look. A short fat man in a uniform had already grabbed the handle to her rollie and was leading it across the tiled lobby, the suitcase's wheels clicking each time they passed over grout. She had to hurry to keep up. Even though it was past one in the morning, music and laughter spilled from the hotel lounge. She could see tall women with long hair hanging on the arms of grinning guys dressed in shorts and Hawaiian shirts with sunglasses perched on their foreheads.

She tipped the bellman and quickly ushered him out of the room. As soon as he was gone, she pulled open the double doors that led onto a small balcony. The smell of the sea was strong and she could hear the waves. There was no moon and the stars looked like ice pick holes. Caroline wanted to reach up and grab the handle of the Big Dipper and pour herself a cup of infinity.

The bed was soft, but not too soft, and the crisp sheets smelled like they were line dried in the sun. Tomorrow she would have to find a cheaper place to stay, but tonight she wanted to fall asleep to the pulse of breaking waves so she left the doors to the balcony open.

Something brushed her skin and then began tugging her. She tried to push it away, but it was as if she were encased in thick, heavy sludge and her arms and legs made of cement. Whatever it was kept tugging and finally yanked her into consciousness. Caroline blinked. "Frida? Do you need to go out?" And then she remembered where she was. The noise that tugged her awake sounded like a keening animal. She slipped out of bed and went to the open double doors. The noise grew louder. Caroline stepped outside. A naked woman bent at the waist was gripping the railing of the balcony next to hers. Her breasts dangled over it. A man with his unbuttoned Hawaiian shirt stood behind her, his sunglasses still perched on his forehead, his hands gripping her hips as he thrusted. He grinned when he saw Caroline. The woman keened even louder.

Caroline quickly retreated into her room and closed the doors. She got back into bed and put a pillow over her head, but she could still hear the woman's cries and the slap slap of skin.

*

Rapping on the door and a sing-song voice calling "Housekeeping" woke Caroline. "*No gracias*," she called back. She reached for her phone to check the time and then remembered she'd left it turned off when the plane touched down to prevent Greta from using Find My Phone to trace her; both numbers were registered under her family plan. Caroline counted her money, got dressed, and went downstairs.

The receptionist from last night was behind the front desk. His hair was still perfectly coiffed, his breath a cloud of stale tobacco smoke. "How was your sleep? Are you going to extend your stay with us?"

"I don't know yet, but can you call this driver for me and have him pick me up?"

"It is better if you use one of the hotel's. They are to be trusted. I'll have one meet you out front."

"I'll trust my own decision, thank you very much. Just call him, please?"

Fifteen minutes later she was in the backseat of Jorge's brown Nissan. "Do you know where I can buy a SIM chip for my phone?" she asked.

"*Sí, sí.* I told you. *Lo se todo. Mi amigo* has a store. He sell you one and put it in, you want. *Más barato.* You save lotta money."

"And after that, can you take me to a bank?"

"There plenty *bancos.* What you need? Change money? *Mi amigo* change it for you. He give you better rate."

"Thanks, but I'll use a bank."

"Hokay. You got other things you need doing, hire me for all day. *Es mejor.* I tell you what. Special deal. Hundred dollars."

"That's too much."

"You tough negotiator, *señorita.* Hokay, hokay. Special deal for you only. Fifty dollars. You gonna spend ten going and ten coming back to hotel anyway."

Caroline paused. She hadn't eaten since lunch the day before. "Do you know a good restaurant?"

Jorge laughed. "This is Mexico. Lotta good restaurants but none as good as *mi madre's*."

*

Jorge didn't mention that his mother lived in a fishing village called Lo Sereno twenty miles north. When he steered the Nissan out of Zihautanejo, Caroline grew alarmed.

"Where are you taking me?" she said, clutching her phone with its new SIM chip.

"*Mi madre's*. You pay for all day, so we go today so you don' pay more tomorrow. *Es mejor*."

Caroline settled back in the seat that was covered in a red, white, and green striped woven blanket. So far, Jorge had done what she'd asked. He'd taken her to the little store that sold everything from beer to mangos where the owner swapped the SIM chip and showed her how to dial local numbers and the U.S. too. The first call she made was to her mother who lived in a Sacramento suburb.

"I almost didn't answer, what with all the numbers that showed up on caller ID," her mom said. "Where are you?"

Caroline told her she was in Mexico, but not the city. "I've ended it with Greta," she said.

"What were you thinking?" her mom said. "She's the best thing ever happened to you since you dropped out of the culinary academy."

"But I wasn't leading my own life. I was following hers."

Her mom's sigh signaled she was also rolling her eyes. "You think your dad and me never felt that way? That's what love is all about. It's always give and take. I bet if I called Greta she'd say the same thing. Call her right now and let her know you didn't mean it, otherwise how are you going to support yourself? You don't want to be a waitress all your life."

"I won't call her. I can't. It's over."

"Then I'll call her. She must be worried sick about you. I

know I am."

"Don't."

"Don't call her or don't worry?"

"Both."

"Well, at least tell me what city you're in. All those things you see on the news. Drugs, murders, and everything. I need to know you're safe."

"I am. I need your help with some banking. I have the five thousand dollars Grandpa left me when he died. It's still in that savings account you opened for me. If you transfer it into my checking account, I can withdraw it on an ATM."

"Why didn't you do it yourself when you decided to throw your life away?"

Caroline took a deep breath. "I didn't throw my life away, Mom. I'm taking it back. Come on, I really need your help."

"I thought you were saving that to open your own restaurant?"

"I was. And this is part of it."

"A restaurant down there? Are you crazy?"

"Mom, please. I can't transfer it online or even over the phone because they're two different banks and those accounts aren't linked."

"Well, if you're sure about this, but I still think you're making a big mistake walking out on Greta. She's a lawyer, for god's sake. That always gave me something to say to Ginny when she bragged about her daughter marrying a plastic surgeon. That woman, honestly."

*

The muffler on Jorge's Nissan sparked when he turned off the paved highway and the skeleton family rattled even louder as the car bounced down a dirt road. "*Bienvenidos a Lo Sereno*," Jorge said. "Welcome to Lo Sereno. It mean in English 'tranquil.' You know, *placido*, chill. That how the rappers say it, chill? I hope you hungry because the food *es la mejor*."

The rutted road led to a row of low slung stucco buildings, each painted a different color. Jorge parked in front of a blue one with the words *Restauranté Francesca* lettered in gold in the window. The interior was small and cramped with a half-dozen tables covered with colorful vinyl table clothes, some with parrots in the design, others with cactus. Two of the tables were occupied.

"*Mama*," Jorge called. "*Traje un cliente.*" He turned to Caroline. "She don' speak much English. I tell her I bring a customer. Sit down. She bring you lunch. Don' worry about any menu. She choose for you."

A woman came out from the kitchen in the back. She didn't look much older than Jorge and wore a white apron with a colorful hem of embroidered chile peppers.

"*Mama, quiero presentarla señorita Carolina*," Jorge said.

"It's Caroline," Caroline said to him.

"*Sí*, what I said, but you're in Mexico now. And this is *mi madre, señora* Flores, but you can call her Francesca."

Caroline shook Francesca's hand. She could feel a cook's scars made by knives, flames, and hot pans.

"*Con mucho gusto*," Francesca said.

She returned to the kitchen. Caroline asked if Jorge was going to have lunch too.

"*Sí*, but in the back. Did I tell you *mi madre* is the best cook in all of Mexico? *Ella es la mejor.* After you eat, I take you back to your hotel unless you got someplace else you wanna go. How you say, I'm still on the clock." He grinned. "Hokay?"

Jorge hadn't exaggerated his mother's cooking skills. Caroline couldn't believe how hungry she was, but she took the time to savor each bite. The handmade flour tortillas were freckled to perfection. The combination of crab stuffed in blackened poblano chiles had her oohing and ahhing. The diced onions, jalapenos, and tomatoes in the salsa topping the pinto beans were so fresh they snapped when she bit into them. A mole sauce drizzled over a juicy chicken breast crisscrossed with grill marks had hints of cinnamon, clove, and chocolate. Caroline thought if she could cook food this good, she'd have them lining out the door and Yelping five stars.

Jorge cleared the plates after she mopped the last of the mole with a tortilla. "You like? I told you you would. You got sweet tooth, you like some *postre*, or you wanna go back to Zihuatanejo now?"

"I'm going to walk around town first and see the sights and maybe go down to the beach."

"Hokay, I be your guide. No extra charge."

"I'd rather go by myself. How about I meet you back here in an hour?"

"Hokay, but I gotta advise you there lotta dog in this town. Some not so nice. Not like dog you see on TV. You see dog coming, you say, *"¡Mal perro. Vete mal perro!* And you say it like you mean it. Go away bad dog. He don' listen, you pick up rock and throw it. You don' wanna get bit."

It didn't take long to walk the length of town. There was a grocery store, souvenir shop, bar, and another restaurant. None caught Caroline's interest, so she didn't bother to go inside. The dogs she did see were asleep, some in the shade, some in the middle of the road. None barked, none approached. She followed another dirt road down to the beach. Wavelets lapped a crescent of white sand while large waves broke along a rocky point. A couple of surfers were riding them. Caroline sat on the sand to watch. Their boards left white zigzags on the open faces as they carved turns and raced the collapsing tubes. The pair's shouts carried over the water as if they were standing right next to her. She could feel as well as hear their hoots and hollers.

A row of houses fronted the beach. *Ranchera* music was coming from one. The medley of polka and country western made Caroline think of last night's cab ride from the airport. It seemed like a long time ago. She ran her tongue over her teeth. She could still taste the flavors of lunch. The spices had infused life into simple ingredients.

Caroline sensed movement behind her and glanced over her shoulder. A yellow dog was coming toward her. She leapt up and yelled. The dog immediately dropped and whimpered. Caroline saw that it was a female. Her ribs showed and her yellow fur was dirty and matted. The tip of one ear was torn and the flap sported fresh scabs in the pattern of teeth marks.

Caroline had never seen mange before, but she was pretty sure that's what the dry patches on the yellow dog's hips were.

"Go away. I don't have any food for you." She remembered her high school Spanish. "*No tengo comida.*" The yellow dog squirmed forward and whimpered. "Go away. *No tengo nada. Vete perra. Vete.*"

Caroline started walking backwards, keeping her eye on the yellow dog who started crawling after her. Every time Caroline glared, the dog would cower. After a few yards, Caroline turned and walked faster. She thought of Frida. They had gotten the little Chihuahua as a puppy. She was so small she could fit in the palm of Caroline's hand. Frida lapped milk out of a saucer like a kitten, turned her nose up at kibbles, and would only eat one brand of canned food. The night they brought her home, Greta fashioned a bed out of a shoe box and put a dish towel in it. She placed the box next to her side of the bed.

"We have to be firm," Greta said. "If we give her an inch, she'll take a mile."

Caroline agreed, but after Frida whined for ten minutes straight, she said, "Can't we bring her up just for a few minutes? She's never slept alone before. She's always been part of a litter."

"Don't be such a softie," Greta said. "If we do that, she'll want to sleep up here every night. Put a pillow over your head. You'll thank me later."

Caroline did and eventually fell asleep. When she awoke, she discovered Frida snuggled between Greta and her. "What happened to your rule about no dogs in the bed?" she said.

Greta stroked Frida's head. "She's not a dog, she's a puppy."

From that night on, the Chihuahua never slept anywhere else.

When she reached the road to town, Caroline looked back. The yellow dog was skulking behind. She didn't waste her breath telling her to go away. She had something much more important to discuss with Francesca.

*

The next morning, Caroline checked out of the hotel and Jorge drove her back to Lo Sereno. His mother lived in a house on the beach and had said yes when Caroline asked if she could rent its *casita*. Francesca also agreed to teach her how to cook her favorite dishes.

Jorge's moustache couldn't hide his smile as he carried Caroline's suitcase inside the *casita*. "You like? Look, you got a view of *la playa* better than hotel. *Es la mejor.*"

"It's perfect," she said.

"*Mi madre*, she very happy you gonna live here. An' not just because you pay her money. When you ready to learn her cooking, just go to the kitchen. *La cocina*. Hokay, I gotta go back to work. *Adios.*"

As soon as Jorge was gone, Caroline set out to make the *casita* hers. She unpacked her suitcase and put her clothes in a dresser that had been painted ocean blue. She spread a bright bolt of fabric she'd bought before leaving Zihuatanejo and spread it on the bed. She'd also snipped a stalk of crimson bougainvillea from the hotel's garden and now arranged it in a plastic water pitcher on the nightstand which was also painted the color of the water lapping outside her door.

"*Casa Dulce Casa*," she said.

Francesca was already at the stove when she arrived for her first lesson. Jorge had told Caroline she'd been cooking ever since she was a little girl. She got her start helping her mother run a food stand alongside the highway. It was nothing more than a *palopa* with a couple of plastic tables and chairs out front. Francesca and her mom cooked over a propane one burner. They made *tacos, empanadas*, and *tortas* for passing truckers and the occasional tourist. Bottles of soda and beer were chilled in a plastic tub filled with ice. After her mom died, Francesca used her savings to rent the storefront in town and open the restaurant. She worked seven days a week, 14 hours a day, except for Sunday mornings when she took a couple of hours off to attend church.

Francesca began by teaching Caroline the proper way to

make beans. The secret, she said, was not to pre-soak them. She held up a stalk of green leaves. "*Esto es epazote. Frijoles con epazote, no pedo.*" And she imitated a fart and brushed the echo away with the herb. They both laughed.

Francesca scooped dry beans from a straw basket and spread them on the counter where she quickly picked out pieces of dirt and small rocks. Then she rinsed the beans and placed them in an *olla*, a clay pot glazed on the outside. She added water, bacon grease, epazote, onions, garlic, lime juice, and dried chiles. "*Sin sal. No por veinte minutos.*" And she held up both hands and flashed her fingers twice to show how long until salt could be added.

With the pot of beans set on a low boil, Francesca next taught Caroline how to make table sauces. "*Hay una salsa para cada plato.*" A sauce for every dish. "*Ranchero, verde, pico de gallo, tomatillo salsa, adobo con ancho chiles, mole pablono.*" Caroline kept asking how much of this and how much of that for each one, but Francesca answered by holding up a tomato or a chile. "*Un pellizco aquí un pellizco allí.*" A pinch here and a pinch there. Caroline grew frustrated until she realized Francesca didn't use a recipe book. She cooked with her senses.

By the time Caroline said good night, her feet were aching like they used to when she worked a long shift waiting tables in a trendy San Francisco restaurant. But it was a good ache, satisfying and well-earned. When she neared the *casita*, she saw the yellow dog. She'd been laying near the door and got to her feet. Caroline tensed and glanced at the ground for a rock, but the light shining from the *casita's* window was too dim to see.

"*Vete perra,*" she said. "Go away."

The mangy dog hung her head and wagged her tail. Caroline was too tired to chase her away. She slipped past the cur and fell into bed.

*

Every day Caroline would wake at sunrise, ignore the yellow dog sleeping outside her door, and walk to Francesca's kitchen. The dog usually followed. She would wait outside the restaurant for Caroline and then follow her back to the *casita*.

Caroline never fed her, never even put out a bowl of water.

On Wednesdays and Saturdays, Caroline accompanied Francesca to the open market held in the town square. It was a chance to meet people who lived in Lo Sereno, the farmers, fishermen, and ex-pat surfers and artists. She learned by observing how Francesca picked out fresh ingredients. While the restaurant owner clearly favored certain vendors, she'd pass them over in a heartbeat if another had fresher or better goods. To Caroline, pinto beans sold at two different stands looked identical, but not to Francesca. She would plunge her hands deep into an open 50-kilo burlap sack, pick out a couple of beans and roll them between her fingertips and bring them to her nose for a sniff. She tested carrots by snapping them in half and listening for crispness. She'd thump melons; a hollow sound meant it was ripe. She'd stick the tip of a knife into the paddle of a prickly pear cactus and then lick the blade to check for flavor.

In the kitchen, Caroline graduated from student to helper. She sliced and diced vegetables, stirred pots, made soup stock, and replenished the spicy table sauces. Francesca gave her a special compliment when she showed particular skill at grilling thin strips of hangar steak for *carne asada* without burning the edges or drying out the meat.

Days turned into weeks and then into a month and then another. One Saturday, Francesca entrusted Caroline with a special assignment. Jorge and his family were coming to the restaurant to celebrate his daughter's birthday and she planned to close the restaurant early for a special meal. Her menu called for grilled whole fish with an ancho-tamarind marinade, spicy red rice, and a black bean, corn, and cilantro salad. For dessert there would be a traditional *tres leches* birthday cake topped with strawberries. While she baked the cake and readied the ingredients for the rest of the dishes, Caroline was to go meet Francesca's favorite fisherman down where the local fleet launched their pangas. He'd been instructed to provide Caroline with the best of his early morning's catch.

She set off down the beach as the morning sky blued. The

air was still cool and the sand untrampled. It squeaked beneath her bare feet as she walked. She didn't have to turn around to know the yellow dog was following at a respectable distance. There was only one panga on the beach when she arrived at the launch. The 20-foot-long skiff was red and named *Santa Catalina*. The fisherman's name was Suerte and he and his son Nacho were fiddling with its outboard motor.

"*Buenos dias,*" Caroline said. "*¿Tienes pescado para señora Francesca?*"

Suerte looked at the sand. "*Lo siento, señorita, no tenemos.*"

"Oh," she said. "*¿Por que?*"

Nacho, who was twelve and wore a T-shirt with a faded portrait of Pelé on it, replied in English. "The motor no start. We not gone fishing yet."

He turned to his dad and said something in Spanish. Suerte nodded. "*Sí, sí.*"

"He said you come fish with us," Nacho said. "That way you choose what you wan'. *Muy frescos.* Very fresh."

Caroline had never been fishing in her life, much less out on the ocean in a small open boat with a suspect outboard.

"What about the motor?" she asked.

Nacho grinned. "It fix now. Le's go. It be okay."

Caroline hesitated. She thought about all the mistakes she'd made in her life. The regrets. The missed opportunities. She thought of Greta always pushing her to try the things that she liked to do. Skiing, dancing, riding horses. As Caroline looked at the boat, she knew that if she couldn't figure out how to let her dreams outrun her memories, she'd never be free of the past and find what she wanted.

"Why not?" she said. "*Vamanos.*"

Suerte and Nacho dragged the panga into the shallow water and held it still as she clambered over the gunwale and sat on the middle thwart. They pushed the skiff toward the surf and jumped in. Suerte pulled the starting cord. Once, twice, and on the third time it caught. The outboard coughed and sputtered to life. The prop began to churn and they were soon plowing through the whitewater and up and over the cresting waves.

The spray stung Caroline's face and she laughed when she tasted the salt on her lips. When they cleared the surf line and reached the kelp beds, Suerte cut the motor and heaved a block of cement tied to a yellow nylon rope over the side. Nacho opened a greasy paper bag and pulled out strings of fish guts. He began baiting hooks to lines weighted with old spark plugs. He handed a line to Caroline and told her to wrap the end around her hand.

"No fishing rod?" she asked.

He laughed. "*Solo manos*. Only hands."

Sunlit sparkles dancing on the water were dazzling and Caroline soon lost track of time. The boat bobbed gently. The sun on her shoulders baked away the lingering chill of the rainy night she'd told Greta that love could no longer hold her. Memories of their first date, the first time they'd made love, shopping for groceries together, and taking Frida to the vet took on a hue of photographs turned gauzy with the passage of time. She would always remember them with fondness, but no longer regret or longing.

A jerk banged her wrist hard against the gunwale and brought her back to the moment.

"Ouch," she cried and brought her hand up fast.

Suerte and Nacho both began yelling instructions. When she finally hauled the fish out of the water and plopped it in the boat, Nacho whistled appreciatively and Suerte grinned.

"*Bueno*," he said. "Le's eat."

Nacho unhooked the fish. Its skin was the color of a sunset. The boy slapped it on the thwart and filleted it before it had time to flap its tail. He cut the meat into dice-sized chunks then pulled out a plastic bag already filled with chopped onions, cilantro, and diced jalapenos. He dropped the chunks into the bag, sliced a couple of limes in half and squeezed them over the contents. Then he twisted the end of the bag and shook it.

He held it out to Caroline. "You want to try? See how fresh?"

She reached into the bag and took a pinch and tossed it into her mouth. The *ceviche* was both sweet and spicy. She ate some more and then some more. Nacho smiled. Suerte reached under his thwart and pulled out a plastic bucket containing clear glass bottles of beer surrounding a chunk of ice that resembled an iceberg dirty with glacial till. He handed one to her.

Caroline took a sip of the cold beer and looked out to sea. A line of brown pelicans flew by. A seagull circled overhead. She couldn't wait to put her hook back in the water and catch another fish.

By noon they had caught a dozen and Suerte steered the *Santa Catalina* back to shore. He cut the motor and pulled up the prop when they reached shallow water. Caroline was the first to jump out and helped push the panga onto the beach. The water was warm and the sand oozed between her toes. She couldn't remember ever feeling so alive.

*

Jorge and his family were already at the restaurant when Caroline arrived. The taxi driver was sitting at two tables pushed together with his three daughters who were braiding fresh-cut flowers into hair garlands. The little girls wore matching frilly white dresses. The youngest was named Margarita Elena and it was her sixth birthday. She was having trouble sitting still. Her black patent leather shoes kept up a steady beat as she clicked the heels together.

Introductions were made amidst lots of giggling. Caroline returned the girls' laughter and told them she was very pleased to meet them. Then she carried the catch to the kitchen where Francesca appraised each fish with a discerning eye and a finger poke to the belly. She spread the dorsal fins and watched to see if they would fold close or stay open like a fan. Closed was good, open meant they'd gotten too dry. She smelled them from head to tail.

"*Muy bien, Carolina. Estos son muy frescos.*" Francesca tapped the corner of her eye. "*Ahora eres un pescador y un concinero.*"

Caroline didn't need a translation to know she'd been proclaimed a fisherman as well as a cook. Jorge's wife wore a big smile and an apron over a shiny red party dress. She fetched a clean apron and tied it around Caroline's waist.

The women chatted while they cooked and then ferried platters to the table. The girls were wearing their flower garlands and they'd made ones for their mother, grandmother, and Caroline too. Margarita Elena stood on a chair to place the flowery crown on her head and insisted they sit next to each other.

When Jorge bowed to lead them in a blessing, he stretched out his hands and his daughters sitting on either side of him grasped them. Margarita Elena took Caroline's hand and Francesca took the other. The circle was complete. When the amens were said, Francesca squeezed Caroline's hand. "*Nuestros amigos son nuestra familia.*" Our friends are our family.

They took their time eating, enjoying each course, talking and telling stories. The older two girls studied English and went back and forth between languages without being self-conscious. They were unabashed at correcting Caroline's Spanish.

Finally, it was time to bring out dessert. Jorge dimmed the lights and Francesca carried out the *tres leches* cake lit with six candles. They sang *Las Mañanitas* to the birthday girl. Caroline had never heard the song before, but she found herself humming along to the verses.

After the plates were cleared and the dishes were washed and the leftovers packed up, Jorge and his wife loaded their girls into the backseat of the dented brown Nissan for the drive back to Zihautanejo. As Jorge was getting in his car, he said to Caroline, "You like the party? You like my family, my town?"

"*Son los mejores,*" she said.

He laughed. "*Sí.* They are the best. And you are *la mejor* too."

Francesca and Caroline looped arms for the walk home. The moon was bright and the light showed the way. They bid each other goodnight at Francesca's front door and Caroline followed the path around to her *casita*. As she neared the porch, she turned to look for the yellow dog. She was skulking behind as usual.

Caroline clapped her hip. "*Ven aquí perra.* I brought you some food. There you go. That's a good girl."

As she lay in bed with a gentle breeze wafting all around and listening to the sound of the yellow dog eating and wavelets scrubbing the beach, Caroline pictured the restaurant she would have someday. It would be a simple place where she would blend spices and fresh food to bring friends and families together. She didn't know where it would be located or when she would open it, nor did she worry. Now that she understood it wasn't important that she had gone but had arrived, she was content just knowing the choice was hers.

THIEF IN THE NIGHT

Bobby Ballena doesn't look like he's spending time worrying about melanoma. His skin is the color of a pair of *huaraches* and his thick curls are streaked from sunshine. We grew up in the same neighborhood and ran together for a while, but this is the first I've seen him since he lit out for Baja three years ago.

"What happen, you mistake saddlesoap for sunblock?" I say.

Bobby looks up from the couch where he's sitting with my wife's feet on his lap and flashes a Halloween grin. "Who died?"

I'm just getting home from the office, but don't bother explaining I'm wearing a suit because I've been in a courtroom all day trying to stop a crew of brogrammers fresh out of Stanford from muscling in on my app. Bobby wouldn't understand. The closest he's ever had to a straight job was back in high school selling popcorn at the theatre. He lasted a week before they realized he was skimming all the little salt packets and pushing them to shut-ins at the old folks' home.

Bobby's rubbing Katie's arches and she has the same look on her face as she does when we're making love or eating crème brulee. I notice she's wearing the purple Pashmina scarf I bought her when we were in Kathmandu. But it can't be. Last time I saw it the scarf was stuffed in the mouth of a tongueless monk the night Bobby and I stole a solid gold Buddha from a temple.

"Bobby bring you a little bread-and-butter gift?" I ask.

Katie nods, all wide-eyed and baby blues. "He remembered

how much I liked the one I lost in Nepal. Isn't he sweet?"

"As Himalayan honey."

Katie spreads her toes and settles deeper into the leather cushions as Bobby starts working her heels. The reflexology chart says they're connected to your pelvis. I know that because she's got a life-size body map pinned to the bedroom wall. It looks like the Africa page in an atlas with all these colored patches on the shoulders, back, and feet. Katie's big on massage therapy. Acupuncture too. Don't get me started on astrology.

"Bobby's been telling me about the school he runs in Cabo," she says, her voice going up and down with her eyelids as he works her soles. "He teaches kiteboarding and lives in a house on the most beautiful beach in the whole wide world."

"Second most," Bobby says. "First is the one you're always looking for."

Katie oohs.

Vintage Bobby. He's always been smooth with the lines. It's how I met Katie. Bobby and I were in Kathmandu for a meet with this antiquities trafficker who chain-smokes Kents and dresses in a jumpsuit and sunglasses like a North Korean dictator when we see Katie and her best friend Laura in a teahouse. They were on some New Age spiritual quest led by a pudgy phony out of Marin County. Bobby sees right through him and decides to cut Katie and Laura from the herd. He tells them his last name means whale in *Español* and he's on a pilgrimage to get in touch with his soul from a previous life when he was a humpback. It's like sprinkling fish food on a koi pond. The next thing you know the four of us are sitting cross-legged on hand-loomed pillows sipping *chai*. That's when the fat phony tries to reel in the girls, reminding them he's holding their passports and return tickets and there are absolutely, positively no refunds. Bobby pulls out a *kukri* he traded a counterfeit iPhone for and starts slicing a mango. Doesn't say a word. Doesn't need to. The wannabe guru's eyes never leave that big curved silver blade. By the time Bobby finishes with the mango, the girls' passports and tickets are stacked next to the teapot. Bobby gives the pudge one of his looks and suddenly it's autumn. Blue and pink rupee notes, green Benjamins, even a couple of traveler checks—they all come fluttering down.

I figure it's no coincidence Bobby shows up bringing a Pashmina like the one I used to silence the monk. Okay, for starters, I didn't know he didn't have a tongue, so it wasn't like I could have known he wasn't going to call for help when I tied him up. Turns out all the monks snip theirs. Goes along with never getting laid and eating nothing but mung beans. Still, you're in the moment you go with your instincts—bind and gag first, check for tongues second. Trust your gut, that's my motto. Like right now. I know the scarf is going to cost me. The question is, how much.

"I'll go make drinks," I say.

I've had a long week and nothing is getting between me and martini Friday. That's the way it is now. Once I was without a care in the world, traveling wherever the next opportunity lay and a hot credit card would take me. Then I fell in love. Now I have to have days with special names to make them stand out. Like "date night." I can't even remember when Katie started calling it that. It was probably Laura who came up with it. She's always telling Katie about these articles on how to make your man feel special. It's a full-time job for Laura now that she's married to one of the richest venture capitalists in Silicon Valley. She's part of his wardrobe along with his Woodside mansion, Tesla, and standing invitation on Larry Ellison's yacht.

I check my phone while walking to the bedroom. Even though I don't expect an email from my lawyer telling me the Stanford punks have settled, I'm still a little disappointed. Running a high-tech business? There are always disappointments. Angel investors throwing their weight around. Employees jumping ship taking your customers with them. Banks calling in your note. Even with online banking there's always another report to print out, a tax form to submit. You're not careful, it's death by a thousand paper cuts.

I hanger my suit and look for my oldest pair of jeans. I pull on a T-shirt with a picture of Bob Marley on it and check the full-length mirror. I yank it off and button up a Tommy Bahama instead. Solid black, no palm trees, no hula dancers. It's more comfortable, plus it covers the extra 10, 15 pounds I put on. Price of working 12-hour days where breakfast, lunch, dinner, and drinks afterward is always a business meeting. It's been like that ever since Katie and I tied the knot and I cut the strings to my old life. I invested everything old Kents and Sunglasses paid us for Little Buddha in two brothers from Bangalore and their algorithm for rating and booking international gentlemen's clubs and escort services, made it through the first couple of rounds of private funding without having to give away the store, then before I can go IPO along come these Stanford geeks with an app that has more social media interfaces and a frequent swinger rewards program to boot. I'm telling you, it's the Wild Wild West in the Valley. There's more honor among thieves than high tech CEOs, and the stress level has you popping beta blockers by the handful. At least with stealing and fencing artifacts you know who's trying to stab you in the back.

I go to the kitchen and whip up a pitcher of margaritas. As the blender whirs, I dump this pink sea salt Katie says is more cardio-friendly onto a paper towel, wet the rims of three thick tumblers, turn them upside down, and twist them into low-sodium drifts the color of pale roses.

The engraved serving tray that was a gift from Katie's parents when we got married in Vegas between turns at the craps table doesn't get past Bobby.

"You've come up in the world," he says with a tone. "No more swilling *chhaang* out of a wooden bowl?"

That gets Katie sitting up with a dreamy smile. "Oh, what I wouldn't give for a taste of Himalayan homebrew. Those were the days. Waking up to first light hitting the mountains? The smell of incense in the temples? The prayer flags fluttering? It was all so magical." I hand her a margarita and she takes a sip, leaving a yellow caterpillar inching across her lip. "Let's go back right now. Just jump on a plane. No more excuses."

Bobby and I exchange glances over pink-rimmed tumblers. To head him off from saying something cute about how that would land us eating rice for the next 20 years, I remind Katie about the lumpy beds in the teahouses, the bug bites, the squat toilets. She arches her brows. They make me think of a pair of minks getting ready to pounce.

"Always Mr. Negativity now." She puts a hand on Bobby's knee. "He's been like that ever since he started his stupid little business. All Mr. Serious all the time. I've always wanted to go back, but time, well, things just got in the way. You know what I mean?"

Bobby pats her hand. "Time doesn't stand still. People do."

Katie oohs again and now she's nodding like he's some kind of navel twiddler. I take a big drink, wishing I'd doubled up on the tequila.

Bobby makes a show of playing with the purple fringe on Katie's scarf. It's made out of wool spun from goats that live on Everest. Hardy little buggers. She's peppering him with questions, like does he still do Tai Chi every morning, but Bobby keeps it vague, his answers slippery as sashimi as he gets her talking about herself. Katie's off and running and I remember the first time we slept together. She admitted she was jealous that Bobby had singled out Laura. Lying together on a musty futon, she kept going on about how Bobby really knew how to talk to women, how she and Laura were lucky to have met him, a world-wise traveler who could help them find what they were searching for. The look on her face now tells me she still believes all that crap about there being a true path. It's all I can do to keep from telling her the truth about Bobby, the only thing stopping me is then I'd have to tell her about me. One of her manuals says there's supposed to be no secrets in marriage, but I'd cut off my tongue like that monk before I'd ever tell her what I used to do for a living.

I check my phone. Still no email from lawyer-boy. "What about dinner?" I say, feeling the tequila starting to nibble at my stomach lining, wishing I'd remembered to transfer the roll of

Tums I always keep these days when I changed out of the suit. "I could fire up the Weber."

Katie goes with the arched brows again. "Didn't you get my text? We're going to Laura and Dexter's."

Okay, I admit it. I didn't see that one coming. I glance at Bobby. He's sitting there with the ends of the Pashmina wrapped around his fingers wearing a big smile and not saying a word because he knows if he opened his mouth I'd see all the yellow feathers.

"Whose idea was that?"

"Mine, silly. I told Laura Bobby's back in town. She's dying to see him."

"I bet."

Katie jumps up and says she's going to get dressed. I turn on Bobby. "You can swallow Tweetie Bird now."

"What are you talking about?"

"How long have you had it in the works?"

"Had what in what works?"

"Whatever it is you're planning."

"Who says I'm planning anything?"

"You think you can just show up after three years and I'll suit up like old times? Wave that scarf around and threaten to tell Katie about sneaking out of the teahouse and hitting the temple, me taking her scarf in case I needed a mask, not thinking I'd have to gag a monk with it."

Bobby waggles a finger. "Which, technically, you didn't need to do."

I slam my tumbler down. "I'm married, for god's sake. I'm legit now. I got a mobile app business. A mortgage big enough to choke a thousand monks."

Bobby shakes his head, his curls as thick as a labradoodle's. "Katie's right. You have become *Señor Negativo*."

"Well, I'm *positivo* you got something planned. This isn't about seeing your old girlfriend. It's about her husband. Who Dexter is. More important, what he's got."

Bobby gives it a few beats, his eyes turning sly. "And from what I hear, it's plenty."

Like I said, Bobby's always been slick with the lines.

"Count me out," I say.

"Okay, but you're the one with the mortgage. You're the one who said for better or worse, til death do you part. I thought earning a little scratch on the side is what husbands are supposed to do."

Before I can tell him where he can stuff it, Katie comes back. She's wearing stilettos and a silk blouse that goes perfectly with that damn purple scarf. Bobby whistles and all I can do is go fetch the car. I drive a Prius now, another one of Katie's ideas, she being big into recycling and saving the whatever. It's so quiet sometimes I got to check to make sure the engine's on.

We get to Woodside and Dexter answers the door. He's a little guy, about a foot shorter than me. Katie says he's got a complex about it, why he's always letting me know he went to Cambridge or Oxford or one of those stuffy colleges where stuck-up British kids go and how he made his first billion picking winners before they were even start-ups. I introduce Bobby not sure how it's going to play, but Bobby sticks his hand out.

"Thank you for honoring me with an invitation to your beautiful home. Now I know why I never stood a chance with Laura." Then Bobby bows like he's the Dalai Lama. "He who wins and honors he who lost is the most honorable of all."

Dexter beams and Katie oohs and I stifle a gag. Laura comes galloping across the limestone tiled entryway like a longshot stretching for the wire at Golden Gate Fields. "Bobby, baby," she cries and throws her arms around him and plants a big wet one right on his lips. Dexter doesn't seem to mind that it goes on for at least a minute, probably because he's blinded by the crown Bobby just set on his pointy bald head. Katie takes Dexter's overcooked noodle of an arm and guides him back into the mansion. Bobby and Laura follow right behind. They're walking shoulder to shoulder, but I can see where his hand landed.

Katie told me Laura chose the interiors herself, but it's clear she worked with a team of designers. The hallway's the size of a hockey rink. Modern art splashes the walls. The living room looks like it was bought off the equivalent of a Buckingham Palace eBay site. The furniture is Gothic, the fireplace big enough to roast a water buffalo.

We sit on overstuffed couches as Dexter goes into this big show and tell opening a bottle of wine. Claret, he calls it, though it looks like a red to me. You'd think he was delivering a baby the way he coaxes the cork out then cradles the bottle. I mean, it takes him longer to extract that two-inch piece of bark than it does a doctor pulling a 9mm slug out of someone's ass. Trust me, I know, having been on the receiving end on account the time Bobby and me got interrupted lifting an 18th century icon from an Old Believers museum in Latvia and the night watchman unloaded his Marakov at us. Luckily, he was half blind from nipping vodka to keep himself warm in what passes for springtime in the Baltics, and even luckier still that we found a doctor who didn't take much persuading to do the operating. Of course, maybe the speed in which he removed the lead from my butt was due to the fact that his usual patients didn't voice many complaints, they being of the canine persuasion. I was in a lot of pain on the ferry ride back to Stockholm, but Bobby kept saying I should be thankful the doc didn't neuter me while he had his scalpel out.

Dexter finally gets the *vino* poured—pardon me, Claret— and Katie and Laura are chatting like they haven't seen each other in years and Bobby's walking around the room, his eyes cataloging the paintings hanging on the walls, the bronze sculptures, the sterling candelabras on the piano that look like they used to belong to Elton John or Liberace. I can all but hear his mental calculator clicking as he figures out the exchange rate on the black market.

To cover, I say, "So, tell me, Dex, what's new on the far horizon?"

Little Lord Fauntleroy never lets you forget he's landed on the cover of *The Futurist* more than once. He waves his goblet like a professor wielding a laser pointer and dives right into a lecture on self-vacuuming carpets, cell phones the size of earrings, and—get this—intelligent TVs. I only catch about half of what he's babbling about, trying to keep an eye on Bobby to make sure he isn't pocketing a Picasso.

"What about you?" Dexter asks. "What is it you're working on again? A children's game?"

I do a good job of not snapping the stem off the wine glass. Right after he and Laura got married I told him about the app, hoping he'd go the second stage of funding, but he turned me down flat. Said he had all his investments already budgeted for the year. Guess that included the G350 he bought the next week and keeps at a private airstrip for high-tech high rollers.

"It's going great."

"Really?" He pronounces it "Ruh-ley." "The word on Sand Hill Road is there is a bit of a sticky wicket with your patents."

The fact he knows that sends my radar into DEFCON 3. Like I say, you got to trust your gut. I go for casual. "You know how it is, Dex. The Valley has more rumors than Vegas has hookers. It's just the usual sort of dotting the i's crossing the t's before we go IPO." I show him some teeth. "I hope you put in a reservation with your broker."

Dexter sports his own wolfish grin as he takes another swish of his fancy wine. I ratchet up to DEFCON 2 and start thinking up an excuse to go call lawyer-boy. Before I get a chance to say anything, a tiny guy dressed in saffron robes and a third eye tip toes in. He's even wearing traditional Nepalese slippers, the ones with the turned-up toes. He makes a steeple with his palms. "Dinner, *memsahib*, is served."

Katie and Laura start clapping and now Dexter looks like he's the one sucking on a canary. Bobby whispers something to the guy in *Español* and gets a dark-eyed look back. He looks over at me and mouths, "Relax, he's Guatemalan."

We follow him to a room that's done up like a tented teahouse, right down to the pounded brass tables and hand-loomed floor pillows. The place is lit by beeswax candles and smoky with incense. Lotus flowers float in glass bowls. A trio is jamming in the corner, one guy drumming a *dholak*, another clanging a pair of brass bells.

Katie gasps. "Oh my god, we've died and gone to Shangri-La."

From now on, I know taking her out to dinner even to a Michelin three star is never going to cut it. "I gotta hit the can," I say.

In a guest bath the size of my house, I speed dial my lawyer. Surprise, surprise, all I get is voice mail, which he'll bill me for anyway. "Call me back," I hiss. "Something's up, I can smell it. The only reason those Stanford pencil necks haven't settled is because someone with pockets a helluva lot deeper than their protectors is bankrolling them, and I got a pretty good idea who."

I head back to dinner, squeezing in beside Katie. Bobby's laying the compliments on thicker than yak butter. Dexter, sitting on a fat pillow that gives him a higher perch than us, is beaming. "I am something of an Asiaphile," he says, none too modestly. A tall geezer in a white turban with a ruby brooch pours our host a spot of wine. The little VC rajah takes a sip, swishes, and nods approvingly. "I do appreciate the many cultures of the Far East having traveled there so often. I own call centers in India, manufacturers in China, logistics in Seoul."

"But you're more cognoscenti than connoisseur," Bobby says, trading the butter knife for a shovel now.

"One does get so much more out of life when one is informed," Dexter sniffs.

"One does," Bobby agrees, suddenly sounding as if he just stepped off a flight from Heathrow. "Knowledge is what separates a collector from a hobbyist. I'm referring to cultural artifacts, of course. Discovery and preservation are foremost. Appreciation of the actual form, well, it really is quite secondary. Wouldn't you agree?"

"Quite." Dexter has his chin raised so high I start thinking of his Adam's apple as a Titleist on a tee.

The turbaned one pours the rest of us wine. Bobby tries it, proclaims the vintage excellent, and says to our host, "Is there a particular religion or tribe you focus on?"

"There may be one or two," Dexter responds coyly.

Bobby winks at me. And there it is. I should've guessed it all along. I don't have time to whisper that whatever antiquity he's planning to snatch from ol' Dex is a really bad idea because someone gongs a gong and a dozen servants dressed in gold silk pajamas troop in hoisting serving platters and bowls.

"Ah," Bobby inhales deeply. "Curried baby goat. My favorite."

No mention of a special collection is made over dinner. There's no reason to. Bobby has picked the right bait and made the right cast. Now all it takes is patience. Dessert is gunpowder green tea ice cream swirled with honey made by the world's biggest bees who buzz around the headwaters of the Ganges.

As Katie digs in she gets an expression like someone's working her heels with an egg beater. "Oh god. Oh god. Yes. Yes," she moans over each spoonful.

After dinner, Katie and Laura scramble from their hand-loomed pillows to head for the powder room. Dexter says, "Would you gentlemen care to join me in the library for an *apre* Cuban and cognac?"

Bobby gives me another wink. "Lead the way."

I'm expecting dark paneling and leather bound books in floor-to-ceiling shelves as Dexter places his palm on a scanner that triggers the locks on a pair of doors that look like they could stop a Mongol Horde. I was wrong about the books. The shelves are filled with Asian antiquities: Ming vases, jade figurines, terra cotta sculptures, lacquer boxes, ivory animals. The hardwood floor is strewn with hand-woven tribal rugs that reflect more colors and countries than Katie's reflexology map.

"Exquisite." Bobby whispers it the same way he does when we're creeping a temple.

Dexter goes to an enormous desk, opens a humidor, and pulls out three cigars the size of the truncheons favored by Ghurkas. We get them going using a gold lighter with the initials CD engraved on it. It's the logo of Dexter's firm, Capital Dexterity. He flicks a switch and the smoke from our stogies forms into a whirling column as dark as a tornado and disappears into a ceiling vent.

"Specially designed centrifuge system," Dexter boasts. "Removes smoke from anywhere in the room, thus eliminating the risk of nicotine staining the artifacts or odor permeating the fabrics."

"Sucks it right up the air shaft and spits it out into the night sky, does it?" Bobby says eyeballing the grate which is about the width of his shoulders.

"Quite. My own design."

"Brilliant." Bobby puffs his cigar until the ember matches the gleam in his eye.

It may be three years since Bobby and I last worked a job together, but I can still read him like a blueprint to an underground vault filled with religious relics. I shake my head to tell him don't even think about it, chances are he'd get stuck in the air shaft dropping down from the roof, that it's sure to be alarmed with an armed response to go with it, but he can't stop grinning. One thing about Bobby, once he gets an idea in that curly head of his, it's like shine on gold.

With Dexter posing like he's Winston Churchill, I take a stroll around. His collection is a couple of couch trips past obsession. There's got to be at least $5 million worth and that's just what a fence like old Kents and Sunglasses would pay before turning around and selling them for 10 times that to private collectors who don't worry about where they came from or how they were gotten.

I circle back and find Bobby and Dexter sitting in wingchairs clutching crystal snifters that could fit a goldfish and a toy sunken ship and pour myself a generous slug. "Here's to you, Dex," I say, swallowing the cognac along with my envy. "Your collection's bigger than the San Francisco Asian Art Museum's."

"One does what one can," he says. "As Robert so eloquently stated, preservation of a culture is paramount. I would also add it is one's duty."

Bobby starts swirling his cognac until the amber liquid is mimicking a hypnotist's spiral. He tilts the snifter so it catches the beam from one of the track lights. The crystal acts like a prism and Bobby makes the fractured lights dance. Dexter can't take his eyes off them.

"Dexter, old chap," he says soothingly. "I'm guessing there's a special *objet d'art* that holds fascination above all others."

Dexter keeps watching the spinning sparkles, but after a few moments puts his cognac down, and walks across the room. A narrow Japanese scroll depicting a samurai and geisha locked in a Kama Sutra clench hangs on the wall. He tugs it like an old-fashioned bell cord signaling a butler it's time for tea. A motor whirs and a panel on the wall slides open. My crystal snifter shatters on the hardwood floor as our old friend, Little Buddha, shiny as he was the day we stole him, smiles back.

On the drive home Katie's snores from the backseat are louder than the hybrid's engine. I jab a chin at Bobby. "How did you know Dexter had it?"

"Kim let me know when it changed hands last year."

"Old Kents and Sunglasses. He still smoking three packs a day?"

"Like a Shanghai steel factory."

"What happened to the original buyer, the Saudi prince or whatever he was?'

"Ran into cash flow problems. Guess the bet he made on launching the first Mid-Eastern online dating site didn't work out so good." Bobby's grin is positively halogen. "I warned you when you put your share of the take into your app startup that high tech's got a short shelf life. Today's must-have gadget is tomorrow's must-take to the recycling bin. Stick with antiquities, *amigo*, the older the better. They never go out of style."

I know he's right, but don't want to admit it. "You'll never get away with it. Dexter's got that place wired to the teeth."

"Don't you mean *we?*"

I slap the Prius' steering wheel. "How many times I got to tell you? I'm legit now. I'm married. Nothing's going to make me risk prison and losing Katie."

"Come on, you know if you don't do it, you're sure to lose her. You're a thief. You stole her heart and now you got to keep stealing to keep it."

I stop arguing and we ride the rest of the way in silence. Katie's all but sleepwalking as I guide her down the hall and deposit her on the bed. My cell pings before I can brush my teeth. It's a text from lawyer-boy: *Confirm ur competition has major nu investor. Settlement a no go. Ur lawsuit a no go. BTW, I resign as ur attorney. Conflict of Interest. My new client, Capital Dexterity, paying me a fatter retainer.*

LOL. He didn't sign off with that, but I know it's what he's thinking. Laugh at this, I say, and text back, *FU.*

I'm hot. There's no denying it. I can see Dexter laughing it up back in his big old mansion. Laughing at me knowing the whole time at dinner my app business was heading for the crapper thanks to him, just another skid mark on the information superhighway. Laughing about how Laura is never going to want for anything. I storm out of the bedroom. I don't bother knocking on the guestroom door. Bobby's sitting on the bed checking over the items in his go bag: a black backpack that holds picks, wire cutters, a coil of rope, and assorted climbing hardware.

"I'm in," I say.

He looks up, expressionless. "You sure?"

"*Positivo.*"

"You know we do this thing, Dexter will know it was us."

"I want him to. As long as all we snatch is Little Buddha there's nothing he can do about it. He can't report it because there's no way he's got any paper on it. No sales receipt. No customs declaration. No *nada.*"

Bobby nods. "You thought through the how?"

"We'll take my Prius. He'll never hear us coming." I see myself belaying Bobby down the air shaft, hauling him back up with our little gold friend, getting away getting 54 miles to the gallon.

"What about spiriting *Señor* Buddha out of the country?"

I grin, feeling the old adrenaline kicking in. "Easy. I know where Dexter hangars his G350 and know a cash only, no questions asked pilot. We'll fly it down to Panama and find a nightclub to meet Kim at where he can smoke all the Kents he wants." I give it a couple of beats. "I got an app for that."

Bobby's smile is wider than the zipper on his go bag. "Fence the statue and the hot plane too. Score two points for our side."

"And afterwards, Katie can fly down and meet me. We're long overdue for a second honeymoon."

"Now you're talking. It's good to have you back, *compadre*. Why the sudden change of heart?"

"You remember that thing the monks who still had tongues were always talking about?"

"You mean karmic destiny?"

"Yeah, what goes around comes around." I pull the Pashmina from my pocket, picturing the look on Dexter's face when he tugs the Japanese scroll and sees the scarf tied in a big purple bow around the pedestal where Little Buddha once sat. "Sometimes Karma's a bitch."

A SPECIAL NOTE FROM THE AUTHOR

Thank you so much for reading *Over Our Heads Under Our Feet*. If you enjoyed this collection of short fiction, please help spread the word by telling your friends and family about it. Also, please leave a review on Amazon, Goodreads, and other online sites visited by readers. It only takes a few minutes and it really does help to know what my readers think. I truly appreciate it. I also hope you'll connect with me on my website where you'll find links to all of my books and blog as well as Twitter and Facebook. I look forward to talking with you.

Thanks,

Dwight
www.dwightholing.com

Acclaim

California Works: Stories
"Dwight Holing's work compels us with the texture of its language, entering us like music and insisting that we feel the story on more than one level as we read it. This is a writer who impresses us with his eye and ear and heart." – *Judson Mitcham, Poet Laureate of Georgia*

The Jack McCoul Capers

A Boatload
"The characters here are delicious, the plot tighter than the proverbial toad's nether regions, the local color spot-on." "A supersonic read." "A great crime novel." – *Amazon*

Bad Karma
"Loaded with dishy one liners. A proficient detective story that keeps the plot turning. Should earn the series a bevy of new fans." – *Kirkus Reviews*

Baby Blue
"Brilliantly authentic. Intelligent prose. Draws you in and keeps you." – *Goodreads*

Shake City
"A lively, engaging narrative." "A fitting addition to the series." "Kept me guessing and entertained throughout." – *Amazon*

Made in the USA
Coppell, TX
07 August 2020

32649160R10095